"I must find my aunt."

Mary kept her voice low as one masculine face after another stared incredulously at her.

Ramirez opened his mouth to answer; at that moment clutching hands appeared behind him and grabbed. Mary gasped. His assailant threw Mary's saviour to the ground, and Ramirez, caught by surprise didn't look to be holding his own.

Mary didn't pause to think. The unfairness of the encounter moved her to action. She entered the brawl and wound up facedown on the ground for her trouble. She then heard a sickening crunch and knew that Ramirez had been badly hurt.

Then comforting arms closed around her, and she opened her eyes. "Ramirez! You're all right," she said softly. "He didn't—"

"No," answered the other, "I did." He signalled over his shoulder where Mary saw the assailant unconscious on the floor.

"Oh," she sighed in relief, nestling even closer.

"Well, missy," said a crisp, familiar voice. "I'll delight to hear your explanation of this."

Mary looked up into the face of her Aunt Winter and fainted dead away.

Books by Margaret Westhaven

HARLEQUIN REGENCY ROMANCE
   MISS DALRYMPLE'S VIRTUE
 6—FALSE IMPRESSIONS
22—SPANISH COIN

SPANISH COIN

MARGARET WESTHAVEN

Harlequin Books

TORONTO • NEW YORK • LONDON
AMSTERDAM • PARIS • SYDNEY • HAMBURG
STOCKHOLM • ATHENS • TOKYO • MILAN

To Joyce Beaman, Iona Lockwood and
Linda Hansen Marlia

Published March 1990

ISBN 0-373-31122-2

CHAPTER ONE

"WHO IS SHE?" asked the dark young man. "The light-haired lady over there, standing next to the wounded officer."

Lord Holland looked across his drawing room. "Ah! A countrywoman of yours, in a way. Half-Spanish. Lady Holland and I met her mother during our first visit to Spain. The year five, I think it was."

"Spanish, is she? I can tell, now you mention it. Something about the eyes. There is no drama, no fire, in the face of the typical English maiden."

"She's half-English for all that. The man next to her is her father," said the baron, choosing not to take exception to his guest's unflattering characterization of British womanhood. "Captain in the Fifth. Invalided out."

"And you invited them here?" The young man looked surprised. A mere captain and his daughter seemed a strange choice for one of the Hollands' exclusive gatherings.

Lord Holland understood. "Those two have claims beyond what meets the eye, Lord Ramirez. The captain's wife was no ordinary Spanish lady. She was Inez de la Rosa."

The young man drew in his breath. "Indeed! And does the daughter know about her mother's work?"

"I think not," responded the other. "Doña Inez could keep a secret. I doubt if even the husband is aware of the full extent, and I would lay you a wager the daughter knows next to nothing. Doña Inez would never have compromised her child's safety."

The count nodded in agreement and continued to stare at the blond young lady, a light of admiration in his eyes.

"PAPA," MARY WINTER was whispering, "I feel terribly out of place."

"Nonsense, m'dear. We were invited," was Captain Winter's gruff response. A haughty footman passed by with a tray of champagne. Though the man didn't even slow down as he neared the Winters, the captain lifted a glass and swallowed the contents at a gulp, shrugging off his daughter's sharp glance. "Well, you ain't old enough for champagne, Daughter."

"And you aren't well enough. You know how weak you felt this morning." Mary continued speaking in a very soft voice, not wanting any of the fashionable people nearby to know that she and her papa were having the next thing to an argument.

"Eh?" said Captain Winter.

Mary shrugged and said nothing further. She kept her hand linked through her father's one arm as if for protection in this strange world. She couldn't imagine what they were doing here in renowned Holland House.

They had been invited, Mary supposed, as a sort of belated compliment to her mother, whom the Hollands had met long ago at the Spanish court. The down-at-heel English military man whom the noble Inez de la Rosa had married, despite his recent valour in the Peninsula, would never have secured an invitation to an affair of this elegance and exclusivity on his own merits.

The social events Mary had so far attended in her grown-up years had been the hectic balls and celebrations which accompanied the Peninsular victories, or the slightly more subdued entertainments designed to relieve the tedium and disappointment of a retreat or a long siege. Never had she attended a party in London, a party missing the frantic flavour of a battle just past or a battle to come. A party, moreover, where all the guests, besides her shabby self and her tatty sire, seemed to be of the first stare of fashion.

Shimmering silks and the flash of jewels and diplomatic orders were a blur before Mary's clear dark eyes as she searched the crowd for someone, anyone, who was not a stranger to her.

"Major Harcourt!" she cried, spotting not far away a familiar face.

A tall man in the uniform of the Fifth, who had been standing alone, looked around and blinked. Mary waved at him.

"That stick Harcourt?" grumbled her father. "I had no use for him when he was the only whist player within a hundred leagues."

"Please, Papa, be nice. He's someone we know. I'm tired of standing about feeling I'm a trespasser," Mary said into her father's ear. She held out her hand to the major, smiling in her frank, friendly way.

Major Harcourt, a tired-looking individual approaching forty whose sensitive, scholarly face seemed to belie his uniform, beamed as he approached Mary and took her hand. His slightly nearsighted eyes twinkled, and he cleared his throat. "Miss Winter! And, er, Captain. My dear young woman, you are as pretty as ever. I'd no idea you were back in England."

Mary shrugged off the compliment to her looks; Harcourt was a courteous man and thus obliged to make some such comment. She had enough nous to realize that her combination of fair hair and dark eyes was not only unusual but unfashionable in English circles and was hardly shown to advantage by the much-worn grey gown she had on. Though she was no longer in mourning, the half-mourning gown was the only thing she possessed that was fit for an evening party. "Papa was invalided home after Salamanca," she said. "We've been here for a few months."

She had barely time to get the words out when her father, apparently deciding that a "stick" who hadn't heard the story of Captain Winter's thrilling charge to the village of Arapile was better than no audience at all, launched forth with a vivid account of the loss of his arm. Harcourt had been in England since before the battle of Salamanca, and he listened politely and even fed the captain a question or two.

Mary acknowledged the major's kindness in listening to Papa, but this highly coloured description of Captain Winter's bravery, which she had heard a thousand times, could no longer thrill her. She returned her attention to the scene about her.

Lady Holland must have invited half of London out to Kensington this evening, at least the half of which inhabited the district bounded by Oxford Street and Piccadilly. And there were many others besides, people whom Mary longed to run up to and address in her mother's native tongue, for they had the look of Iberia about them. Mary let her eyes rest on a stern-looking matron in a lace mantilla and a gown of a mode rarely seen anymore on England's shores. Such a dress did Mama wear in the one portrait Mary had of her, but on Inez de la Rosa the costume had been graceful and elegant, not fussy as it appeared on that unfortunate dame across the room.

Mary's own grey dress, despite its lack of attractions, was in the latest mode. Since coming to England she had refurbished her scanty wardrobe by judicious cutting and reseaming, though taking such trouble with her worn garments had seemed rather like decorating one of the burnt-out cottages she had seen in such numbers in the Peninsula. Her wardrobe was a cross she had to bear, given the present state of Papa's finances; but she found an outlet for her fashion sense in evaluating the sartorial choices of others. Her eyes grew thoughtful as she considered the low-cut red silk gown worn by another of the Spanish-looking ladies. The military chatter of Papa and Major Harcourt ebbed and flowed around Mary without her paying it any heed.

In such a crowd she didn't even notice the darkly handsome young man who was still staring at her.

"Good Lord, sir," said Major Harcourt suddenly, "what's the matter?"

Mary came out of her reverie with a snap. Her father was mopping his brow with a huge white handkerchief. He looked every bit as white as the linen he held in his one hand.

"Papa! It's the fever, isn't it? I was afraid it was coming on."

Captain Winter shrugged as casually as he could in his obviously weakened condition. Mary stripped the glove from her hand and touched her father's forehead, expecting it to feel as clammy as it had looked a moment before. Now it was suspiciously dry.

"Major, he's burning up. Would you be kind enough to call our carriage? It will be Sir Egbert Winter's post chaise. My uncle," she explained. The major made a brief bow and hurried off to do her bidding. "Come, Papa, we're going home." She circled an arm about her father's thick waist in an effort to support him.

"Nonsense, m'girl, I'm right as a trivet," snarled Captain Winter, shaking her off. "There's the supper, Mary my child. The supper! And..." He sighed, drawing his handkerchief once more over his rugged face.

"You aren't in any condition to eat. Come along, Papa."

Captain Winter's stocky figure was decidedly drooping by now, and he slumped against Mary's shoulder, causing her to stagger. She ignored the curious glances around her as she manoeuvred her father toward a nearby door which she knew led to the hall. With any luck, the carriage would be at the front sweep by now.

"Demmed fool carpet," muttered Captain Winter, and in the same breath, he tripped on the edge of the Axminster and sprawled across the floor.

"Oh, Papa." Mary knelt by him, not knowing whether to laugh or cry. Her father's recurring bouts of fever, an illness he had picked up in the East, rarely scared her any longer. Papa always recovered, though he would be uncomfortable for days. The nuisance value of the attacks was still considerable. Why hadn't she simply forbidden Papa to come to this party tonight? She had known he was sickening for something.

The answer was simple. Captain Winter went his own way with no interference from females. Somewhere deep inside her, Mary understood that it was this infuriating quality of her papa's, his stubbornness, which had made her mother, once upon a time, think him exactly the man for her. To a strong personality as Mary knew her mother's to have been, Captain Winter's bullheadedness might have resembled an answering strength.

The immediate problem before Mary, however, was not her parents' reasons for marrying, but how she was to get her father to their carriage. Many of the starched-up strangers near her had stopped to stare at the odd spectacle of a one-armed, middle-aged man in uniform lying on the floor. But not one moved to help, and several pointedly turned their reputable backs, indicating that they thought the problem was an excess of wine.

"Señorita," murmured a low voice in Mary's ear, "may I assist you?"

The accent was charming, the voice well-modulated. Mary looked up into the inky black eyes of a handsome young man.

Dressed in elegant dark evening clothes, he was in his late twenties or perhaps as old as thirty. A very faint scar, whitened with age, stood out on one of his dark chiselled cheekbones. The young man had a forceful nose and a mouth which Mary thought curved rather too intimately; it was not exactly a smile, for it would have been heartless to smile at a lady whose escort lay unconscious, but there was something in the young man's manner which struck Mary as less than respectful. His face was too close to hers; if she hadn't realized she was distraught and therefore unable to judge correctly, she would have thought he was staring at her own mouth in a bold, unseemly way.

"Gracias, señor," said Mary, instinctively lapsing into what she sensed must be his native tongue. "My father is taken ill. We're having the carriage brought round, but he's insensible and I'm afraid I can't manage."

"Allow me, *señorita,"* the gentleman answered. He matter-of-factly reached down to haul the captain up by his one arm. Captain Winter came to life long enough to let out a colourful curse at the strain on his limb. As Mary scurried to his left side and put her arm around him, he went limp again.

The young man, Mary's helper, was very strong, for Mary felt hardly any of Papa's weight. Yet they were moving easily out the double doors and into the hall, where a footman, seeing the strange procession, flung wide the front portal.

The Spanish gentleman, speaking in imperious English, directed the footman to relieve Mary. Another servant, hovering by the stairs, was dispatched to fetch her wrap.

Mary was impressed by her saviour's air of command. She quickly ceded her place to the first footman and gave the second a description of her black velvet cloak.

"Thank you, sir," she said, turning round from this task only to find that the gentleman and the footman were disappearing out the door with Captain Winter between them.

Mary could not hurry out after them into the bitter cold of the November night until the other footman had placed her worn cloak about her shoulders. A light snow was falling. At the front door stood her uncle's carriage, and Major Harcourt, whom she had quite forgotten. He was just backing out of it as she arrived.

"I've seen your father settled, Miss Winter," said the major in his diffident way. "You'll be all right? Or should I escort you home?"

Mary's eyes darted about her before finally coming to rest on the major. "Thank you, sir, but there are plenty of servants at my uncle's to deal with Papa. Is he still in a faint?"

"I fear so, ma'am. I—"

"Major," Mary interrupted, an urgent note in her voice, "there was a dark young man who was helping

Papa out to the coach. What became of him? I'd like to thank him."

Harcourt shrugged. "Him? Some servant came running up to him just a moment ago, jabbering something in Spanish, and the fellow went off with him in a hurry."

"What a shame." Mary's face drooped. "And you didn't know him, sir?"

"Never seen him before, Miss Winter. But if I should meet him again, I'll convey your thanks."

"I would be most grateful." Mary stood on the steps of the chaise, looking down at the major. "It was beyond anything great to see you again, sir, despite the circumstances. Papa will be mad as fire when he realizes his illness interrupted his favourite story."

Harcourt shook the young woman's hand. "Brave as ever, I see. Miss Winter, I wish your father the best of luck. I'm about to return to Spain, so I won't be able to enquire for him, but my thoughts are with you both."

Mary smiled; sincerity rang out in Major Harcourt's voice, and she realized how much she missed the simple honesty to be found in the military. After only a few months in the stilted society of her English relations, she had nearly forgotten how refreshing were the easy greetings and partings among men who might be soon to die.

"My thoughts are with you, too, major, and my prayers," she said softly. She looked after Harcourt's thin, erect figure, hoping that she would see the man again, well and whole.

As the chaise sped through the night back to her uncle's estate in Berkshire, Mary's solicitude for Papa, who moaned and grumbled throughout the jostling trip, helped banish from her mind the thought of any other person.

She spared only one regretful sigh for the handsome young stranger who had helped Papa to the carriage. She wished she had been able to thank him, and she suspected that more than politeness motivated this wish. Had she been able to offer her thanks they might have exchanged names. Perhaps...

Mary shook her head at her own folly. A man of that calibre, an obviously rich young man who moved in diplomatic circles, would never be interested in her.

NURSING CAPTAIN WINTER was a time-consuming task, for he couldn't be left alone, and Mary was unwilling to burden her uncle's servants any more than was necessary. But once the most intense, frightening period of the fever had run its course, nursing no longer took Mary's attention, merely her time. As she sat at her work or tried to read, she recalled to her mind more than once a handsome, chiselled face, an intriguing small scar on a long cheekbone, a pair of black eyes like velvet.

Mary was staring aimlessly out the window into a starry night when Captain Winter stirred on his pillow.

His daughter noticed that the candle had guttered out long ago and that the room was in complete darkness except for the flickering of the small sea-coal fire in the grate. "Papa?" she said softly. He hadn't come to himself yet in the few days of his fever. He had only had several spells of raving, interspersed with fitful sleep. Mary was longing to hear her father speak rationally.

The captain muttered as he tossed back and forth. Mary could barely make out his dark shape in the faint light cast by the fire. "Mine," he moaned suddenly with surprising clarity. "All mine."

"Yours, Papa?" Mary prompted, leaning over the bed to pass a cool, damp cloth over what she was disappointed to feel was still a fevered brow.

Not surprised to receive no answer, she put the cloth back into a nearby basin and relit the candle by the bedside, hoping that Papa was sinking into sleep again, and that this time he would come out of it his old self. Though the loss of his arm had made him belligerent and fussy and the chronic nature of his fevers had made him unfit for battle, Captain Winter had maintained his wits, although living with him was something of a trial.

A couple of days past he had awakened in a rage and accused Mary of selling his missing arm to the Resurrection Men so that the Winters would have some money. He had yelled at a terrified maidservant to call a magistrate while his iron-strong right hand gripped Mary's wrist. She hadn't quite recovered from the shock of that scene.

Captain Winter, the flaring light of the candle revealed, hadn't gone to sleep at all. His light blue eyes were staring at something; not at Mary, but at something far distant.

"Yes, Inez," he murmured, "Mary's. Hang it, woman, a man must try."

"Mary's? Papa, what do you mean?" Mary couldn't help asking. This might be raving, but the words intrigued her mightily.

"Garnets," muttered Captain Winter.

Two seconds later he was asleep, snoring loudly. The fever broke during the night, leaving Mary thankful and eager to question him, when he should return to reason, about what had led him to speak of garnets.

He must have been referring to the garnet necklace which was Mary's only inheritance from her mother. Why should he have claimed it as his own?

CHAPTER TWO

WHEN MARY WALKED into the breakfast room of Woodbank Hall, her uncle's country seat, her step was jauntier than it had been in days. Last night, the first night since Captain Winter's fever had broken, she had gone to bed without dinner and slept until morning in the secure knowledge that Papa was at last truly on the road to recovery. Upon waking she had noted with pleasure that the red lines were gone from her eyes, and she had donned an old black woolen round gown hurriedly, anxious to go downstairs. She was ravenously hungry.

Already at the table were Mary's uncle, Sir Egbert Winter, and his lady. The large sheepdog who was Lady Winter's constant companion looked up briefly from his place at his mistress's feet and lifted a paw in greeting. Mary wasn't surprised that cousin Annabella, the daughter of the house, wasn't yet down; indeed, Mary would have fallen over in a dead faint if her cousin had appeared at the breakfast table. Annabella considered herself a pattern card of fashion, and it was well known that ladies of ton slept until noon.

No such rules of conduct affected Aunt Winter. ''Morning, Niece,'' said that lady, nodding brusquely as she speared a piece of steak from a platter set directly in front of her. Letitia, Lady Winter, was a statuesque woman with a hawklike profile. Upon meeting her aunt for the first time, Mary had not been able to stop herself from asking if Lady Winter were related to the Wellesleys, for the resemblance to the new Marquess of Wellington, in profile at least, was quite striking. As it turned out there was no blood connection.

Her ladyship was attired in a dark blue riding habit, and a battered man's felt hat was shoved onto her iron-grey curls. From the faint whiff of horse which drifted across the room, Mary surmised that Lady Winter had already had her morning ride. "How's that father of yours, child?" Aunt Winter continued in a bracing tone after she had cut into her steak. "Don't stand there; sit and eat."

"He's much better, thank you ma'am," returned Mary, hastening to obey. She filled a plate with buttered eggs, kippers, toast and a slice of ham and sat down at her uncle's right hand. A footman poured chocolate for the young lady on a careless signal from Lady Winter. He had made no motion to serve Miss Mary Winter before receiving the crucial sign, and Mary was not unaware of this telling detail of her position at Woodbank Hall.

Once seated by her silent uncle—for Sir Egbert spent every breakfast time immured behind his newspaper—Mary looked about the elegant, wainscotted room, whose draperies were tied back to reveal a thin autumn sunshine, and wondered why the place still felt so uncomfortable. Part of it was, of course, that

Mary, as well as her father, disliked accepting charity. Woodbank Hall was Captain Winter's childhood home, and many might argue that he had as much right here as his elder brother, Egbert, who, thanks only to the annoying custom of primogeniture, now owned the estate as well as the title of baronet passed on to him by Mary's grandfather.

Mary knew that she and her father had been forced to accept Sir Egbert's kind invitation to make their home with his family until they got back on their feet; they had no closer kin. But living at Woodbank Hall was taking its toll on her pride.

There was that subtle difference which every servant sensed between the indigent relation and the ordinary guest. Papa fared somewhat better in this regard, for several aged retainers remembered him as the flighty younger son of bygone days, a person who truly belonged at the Hall. There was even a ninety-year-old nurse living in a cottage on the property who had regaled Mary with tales of Captain Winter as a boy in leading strings. Mary, whose looks betrayed her half-foreign blood, was suspect as family and doubtful as an Englishwoman. She could understand the servants' reserve, but she didn't know what she could do about it.

She stole a look at Sir Egbert's grizzled head, just the shape of Papa's, barely rising over the top of his newspaper as he held it close to his nearsighted eyes. Uncle Egbert never had much to say for himself, but she liked him. Lady Winter was a pleasant woman, too, in her way. She was delighted with Mary's riding ability, and Mary had learned in her time at Woodbank Hall that a compliment to one's equestrian skill was Lady Winter's highest form of praise.

Then there was cousin Annabella... Mary applied herself in earnest to her breakfast, preferring not to think about that thorn in her side on such a lovely morning.

"Fresh air, my girl, that's the thing," said Lady Winter, peering down the table at her niece. "You're pale as a ghost. I want you out of that gown and into your habit as soon as you've eaten. A good gallop—a sure cure for what ails you." As medical advice this was to be taken with a grain of salt, since Lady Winter was known to prescribe a "good gallop" for every ailment known to mankind with the possible exception of a lying-in.

"Thank you, Aunt, I'd love a ride," said Mary eagerly. "But there's Papa. He's reached the crotchety stage of his illness. He's a dreadful patient, and I've already spent the night away from him. I hate the maids to be bothered—"

"Nonsense. That's why I pay 'em, to be bothered," returned Lady Winter. "And you can carry a message for me into the village if you're determined to make yourself useful. It's about that new brood mare of Squire Evans's. And you can save the footman a trip by collecting some more of that bark stuff your father needs from the apothecary."

Mary hid a smile, wondering how long her list of errands would grow before Lady Winter was through. Only one more task was added; delivering a note to the vicar about a hymn Lady Winter hadn't approved of in last Sunday's service. Mary was free to go as soon as she cleaned her plate.

"Enjoy your morning, my dear," said Sir Egbert when Mary rose to leave the room.

Mary almost jumped. Through her uncle's spectacles, she observed the pair of watery blue eyes which had so unexpectedly appeared over the newspaper. "Thank you, Uncle." Not for the first time, she wished that she and Uncle Egbert could become close. But he was a shy sort of man, and this quality seemed perhaps more pronounced when compared to the determined forcefulness of his wife. When he wasn't hiding behind the newspaper he was in his library. Though there was a general impression about the household that Sir Egbert was a man of influence, nobody was certain how he occupied his many solitary hours, and nobody was interested except for Mary, who was too diffident to inquire.

Dinners, especially company dinners, were visible torture to Sir Egbert, for he had to make do without the crutch of the printed word and be civil to his guests. Mary resolved, as she had before, to find some way to be useful to her uncle. Perhaps he wouldn't be too alarmed if she offered to catalogue his books; that might be a way into his trust and esteem. Having few relations, Mary longed to be a friend to her only uncle.

For now she simply smiled at him, curtsied to Lady Winter—who still frightened her a bit, as that lady had a habit of frightening everyone in the world—and hurried into the wood-panelled Elizabethan hall, hung with highly polished antique weapons, and swiftly ascended the intricately carved oak staircase. At the landing Mary carefully closed behind her the elaborate small gates, originally designed to keep the family dogs of the late sixteenth century out of the upper reaches. They were still in use, serving to dampen the enthusiasm of Lady Winter's hunting spaniels, though Mack the sheepdog merely hopped over the picturesque barrier on his way to his favourite lounging spot by his mistress's bedroom fireside.

There was another set of stairs to navigate before Mary reached her own room, a simple chamber with only a gabled window to save it from utter bleakness. Not quite servants' quarters, but not quite the best room in the house. Mary considered her little haven a perfect reflection of her ambiguous position. She knew her aunt and uncle didn't mean to browbeat her by sticking her in what had probably once been the governess's room, for most of the larger bedrooms stood in desperate need of refurbishing. After Papa had been settled in the slightly musty quarters of his youth, Mary had been happy enough to accept a small guest chamber without a smoking fireplace or any of the other disadvantages of the grander rooms.

She crossed to the cupboard of her sanctum and drew out her riding habit, a much-mended garment she loved dearly. It had been her travelling costume for all of those retreats and advances on the Peninsula. Black, like the gown she took off, the close-fitting habit still flattered Mary's figure as it had the first day she put it on. The mere touch of the threadbare velvet took Mary back in time to the summer of 1809.

"You see, you do have a figure," her mother had said in triumph, speaking from the bed where she was confined in the last stages of the consumption which was soon to carry her off. Doña Inez's rich voice was weak, but she retained her spirit and argumentativeness to the last. "A late bloomer, that has been your trouble. But no longer."

Doña Inez was referring to the spots, flatness of chest, and general lankiness of figure which had plagued Mary's adolescence and made her coming out into society completely unnoticed. Miss Mary Winter didn't attract young men, and that was that. But when Mary reached nineteen on the very day the box containing Doña Inez's new riding habit came from the Portuguese dressmaker, the sick lady had insisted her daughter try it on. Mary's spots had vanished during the previous year, leaving her face almost attractive, in the girl's cynical view. And now, wonder of wonders, the black riding dress revealed that the problem of a flat chest and nonexistent hips had also flown while Mary was not looking. She had her mother's lovely figure.

Holding up the train of the habit, Mary had twirled about her mother's room, wishing their Lisbon lodgings were four times as big. It was impossible to dance in wide enough circles to interpret her joy at this amazing discovery. "Mama," she said, kneeling by the bed. "Perhaps I won't be an antidote." The last word, spoken in English, was an expression picked up from Papa.

Doña Inez, with her customary asperity, replied that her daughter would be as beautiful as she believed herself to be and set Mary to reading from her favourite Góngora.

Three years later, Mary straightened the same black velvet riding habit, added a mannish top hat given her by Lady Winter, which she had softened by attaching a lace veil, and made a face at herself in the mirror. Did she believe herself to be beautiful, as Mama had instructed?

Whatever brief trust she had had in her own attractions was never put to the test; mourning for Doña Inez had followed shortly upon the heels of Mary's discovery that she might not be an antidote. And though she had met some admiring young officers in those hectic years of Papa's service in the Peninsula, men of good family, whether Spanish or English or Portuguese, were as reluctant as they would have been in peace time to embroil themselves with a penniless young woman of quality. Not to mention that Doña Luisa, the stern elderly duenna inherited from Mama, was on hand at all times to ensure that no young man overstepped his bounds and that Mary's life continued to resemble more closely that of a Spanish than an English girl.

Mary was not so much modest as mistrustful when it came to her looks. She shrugged off what compliments she received during the campaign by telling herself that anyone would look good to those poor officers who hadn't seen home in years and must miss their sweethearts terribly. Wellington was notorious for allowing leaves only in the most extenuating of circumstances.

Well, if not precisely beautiful, she was *not* an antidote, Mary assured her image in the glass. She gave herself an encouraging nod and left the room.

When she reached the floor below she peeked in on Papa. His was a large, old-fashioned chamber, panelled ornately in oak and hung with threadbare tapestries, as were many of the rooms in the manor. A window embrasure lined with leaded glass panes was the focal point of the bedroom, for it looked out on a terrace which in summer was a riot of roses, or so Mary had been told. In November the view was still amusing, for one might gaze upon all the evergreen topiary shrubs and mazes of the quaint garden.

Mary approached the highly carved tester bed. The curtains had been drawn back, and Papa was propped up on the pillows, a tray across his lap.

"How wonderful, Papa! You're up and eating," she greeted her rumpled-looking sire.

He glared at her. "Call this eating?" He pushed at the tray, nearly dislodging the bowl it held.

"You're practically well already if you're being difficult," said Mary gaily. She removed the tray from the danger zone. "Gruel, I see. I'm glad the cook has taken my instructions to heart."

"I knew you were responsible," muttered Papa.

Mary beamed, so glad to see him returned to reason that she didn't even care that he was being grumpy. Suddenly a question which had been plaguing her was on her lips.

"Papa, when you were ill and raving you mentioned something about my garnets. At least I assumed you referred to my garnets, for first you said they were yours, then that they were mine. What did you mean?"

Captain Winter's eyes bulged under slightly beetling brows. "What sort of fool notion is that, my girl? Why would I speak of female fripperies? Surely a raving man's got better things to think of."

Mary imagined that his words were a touch furtive, and that his light eyes shifted quickly away from her searching gaze. "It was so interesting," she said with a shrug. "You seemed to be talking to Mama."

"I'm always talking to your mother," said Captain Winter. He nodded across the room to the mantelpiece. "She's right here, ain't she, and wearing the garnets, come to that. Perfectly natural."

Mary had to turn to the portrait of Doña Inez, done by Goya in the early years of the century when the family had been separated. Mama had held a position at the Spanish court while Mary was at a school in Kensington and Papa had served with General Wellesley in India. There stood Doña Inez, the epitome of Spanish beauty from her tumbling cascade of black hair to the dainty red shoe which peeked from under her flowing white skirt. Doña Inez's head was bare, and she stood staring straight into the viewer's eye with an odd expression which Mary recognized perfectly. She had seen that look in Mama's dark eyes time and again when a certain small girl had got into mischief. Severity tempered by amusement, that was the expression. Señor Goya must indeed be a genius to have captured it. At Doña Inez's throat sparkled an ornate garnet necklace, Mary's inheritance.

When Mama had given the garnets to Mary, she had cautioned her daughter to keep them safe. There was something special about them, Doña Inez had said, something which would be revealed to Mary in time. And now here was Papa, appropriating the garnets for himself, though only in his dreams. Mary nearly shivered, seeming to hear Mama's warning. *Keep the necklace as safe as you would your virtue, my daughter.*

"In your fancy, Papa, it was she who reminded you that the garnets belonged to me," she said in a light, conversational tone, trying not to betray her real interest.

"She would," muttered Captain Winter. "Always one for reminding a fellow of this and that, was Inez." He sighed, a deep, rattling sound. "I miss that woman."

Mary set the tray down on a nearby table and impulsively gave her father a hug. "I miss her, too." Though she could feel in her bones that there was more to his raving about the garnets than Papa would admit, she decided to drop the subject for the present. He was still ill, and he didn't need to be plagued with questions in his condition. Papa only became maudlin about his wife's death in his cups or after one of his bouts of fever.

"Would you like me to play you a game of backgammon later, Papa?" Mary suggested.

Captain Winter barked out something confused about being a broken man and unfit for anything but board games, which Mary interpreted as an agreement to her suggestion. She knew he would rather be wintering in Portugal with the army than anything; sometimes all attempts to amuse him fell flat, but she must continue to try.

"I know backgammon isn't the war, sir, but you're rather stuck with it, aren't you?" She kissed his cool forehead.

"You're not a bad daughter, I'll give you that much," grumbled Papa. A half smile was visible under his bristling military moustache.

Having straightened her father's bedclothes and rung for a maid to take away the tray, Mary bade her sire good morning and went on her way down the corridor. Captain Winter's room, like the others in the family wing of the first floor, opened onto a wide gallery with tall, many-paned windows on the side opposite the bedroom doors. Mary's step was light. Papa was better, she was to go riding, and she was walking about in her English family's ancestral home as she had so often longed to do after one of Papa's stories of his Berkshire boyhood. If only she could have persuaded Papa to explain that statement about the garnets! Well, there were other days.

A little smile played about her lips as she hummed a Castillian folk tune, her boots clicking on the polished floor of the gallery.

"Well, what have we here? Escaping from Uncle George? I suppose he can be quite a pest, poor old thing."

Mary looked up. Leaning against the frame of an open bedroom door was cousin Annabella, the usual superior smile on her lips as her eyes went over Mary.

Annabella was a tall, well-rounded young woman of nineteen, with masses of fluffy red-gold hair and eyes the colour of a robin's egg. She dressed in a flamboyant style which a more discerning mother than Lady

Winter might have curbed, and which tended to low necklines and colours too bright for an unmarried girl. This morning was no exception. For a night on her maidenly couch she had chosen a transparent gauze nightrail trimmed with masses of ruffles, each one edged in lace. Mary often felt insignificant beside cousin Annabella, who, despite the fact that she was no beauty, made every head turn when she entered a room in one of her striking costumes, her manner as assured as that of a queen.

Annabella was the living example of one of Doña Inez's lectures on confidence. She thought she was the most beautiful young woman in England, and a surprising number of people accepted her judgement in this particular without considering that she might be a touch overplump, or that her eyes might have a vacant look about them when they were not narrowed in calculation.

"Good morning to *you*, Cousin," said Mary with a touch of sarcasm. Her cousin never bothered with proper greetings.

Annabella's mind, though fairly shrewd at times, was not of the sort to appreciate satire. She didn't catch the rebuke, but nodded pleasantly and beckoned Mary to follow her into her room.

Mary shrugged and did so, though her feet were itching to be off to the stables. Annabella's overtures of friendship were few enough, and in the spirit of wanting to get to know her relations, Mary didn't like to refuse.

Annabella plumped herself down in the middle of her lace-hung bed and smiled sunnily. "You dear creature, I'm so glad I caught you. Going riding, are you?"

"Your mother insisted," said Mary. She took a fragile gilt chair near the bed, wondering what on earth this was about.

"And so she ought. You must be worn out from your nursing duties," returned Annabella. She fluffed out her robes in a favourite gesture.

Mary murmured something noncommittal and silently prayed that her cousin would get to the point before the day was gone.

"I wanted to talk to you about the hunt ball," said Annabella. "It's the first real party of the winter, since the October assembly was cancelled, and I know you won't be going. You won't leave your papa, naturally. No more would I in your place. And I thought that since you wouldn't be attending, you could have no need of your delightful garnet necklace. I've ordered such a lovely gown, a garnet stripe on cream satin, you know, and there's nothing like your necklace among Mama's jewels or mine. It would be a perfect match. Could you?" The light blue eyes looked cajolingly into Mary's.

Mary glanced sharply at her cousin and thought carefully before answering. When she was confident she had the means to disconcert Annabella, she spoke. "But I might be attending, if Aunt and Uncle decide to take me into society. My father is much better, and the ball isn't for weeks. And since the garnet necklace is my only good piece of jewellery, naturally I would wear it myself. So sorry." Mary's idea of cousinly comradeship stopped short of lending her only inheritance from Doña Inez.

She knew that Annabella's request was only made out of harmless vanity, and in a way Mary hated to refuse, but she couldn't simply forget her mother's words to her. She must safeguard the garnets. The specific reason for such care she could not fathom, but she could hardly entrust the garnets to someone like Annabella, a careless fribble who would likely lose them or forget to return them.

A flash of anger crossed Annabella's round face, only to be replaced an instant later by a sugary smile. "I'll ask Mama whether she means you to attend," she said. "No need for you to bother. Do you mean to say you've something suitable to wear, Cousin? I must confess I'm a little surprised."

The allusion to her awful wardrobe might have been uncalled-for, but it was no more than the truth. Mary didn't have a suitable dress to wear to a dancing party, and there was no way she could attend the upcoming hunt ball. Her last muslin ball gown had been thrown out as too shabby and too much washed before she'd left the Peninsula, and even supposing she and Annabella were of a size, which they weren't, Mary doubted that offers of clothing would be forthcoming. By pretending that she might go out into the world, Mary was only trying to tease her cousin a little and make her forget about the necklace.

"Oh, you never can tell what I might find to wear," she said with a wave of her hand, mischievously enjoying the look of consternation on Annabella's face.

"Well, if you don't, may I borrow the garnets?" Annabella's full lower lip jutted out. "You don't understand, Mary. I do so want to impress Mr. St. Charles."

Mary had met this latest adorer of Annabella's when he had come calling at the Hall; he didn't seem the type to be impressed by jewels and finery. A stolid young man, he looked much too down-to-earth. "I'm sure Mr. St. Charles admires you for your fine qualities," said Mary, wishing she dared to roll her eyes. "In any case, you'll have to impress him without my garnets." She got up, nodded at her visibly fuming cousin, and left Annabella's room without another word. Since she couldn't provide the right answer, she assumed that her presence was no longer necessary.

She was riding across the barren fields on her aunt's second-best hack before it occurred to her to wonder how Annabella knew that her cousin Mary possessed a garnet necklace. Mary had never worn it since she had come to live with her English relations, though she had once shown it to her aunt.

"Probably Papa." She shrugged. Captain Winter was a bragging sort of man, and he might well have mentioned the antique garnet necklace his wife had left to their daughter.

Mary forgot about her necklace and her cousin and concentrated, as she often did these days, on the memory of a dark, aristocratic face and a pair of compelling black eyes. Even as she dreamed, she chided herself for her folly. She had seen that young man at the Hollands' party for such a brief moment, and she would never see him again. How silly of her to make him the principal player in her new and vaguely embarrassing fantasies.

CHAPTER THREE

"You're being ridiculous, Mama," said Annabella with a pout. "I assure you Mary doesn't want to go anywhere. She told me she hates society! All I did was inform you that you needn't bother asking her to go to the ball with us, out of regard for the poor dear's feelings. I only mentioned her lack of suitable wardrobe to spare her further embarrassment. Really, Mama, I'm surprised you think a new dress..."

Lady Winter eyed her daughter sharply; so did the sheepdog at her ladyship's feet.

Annabella had never been fond of dogs, despite being raised by such a mother, and she couldn't look at the gigantic Mack with anything approaching affection; at least not enough affection to warm her mother's heart.

Lady Winter shook her head. Annabella was a changeling indeed, hating all forms of sport, refusing to ride at a faster pace than a trot, and now trying to push her cousin into the background. Was it jealousy? She looked at her daughter carefully, trying to make sense of that explanation.

No. Her ladyship had grown fond enough of Mary and thought her a pleasant girl, but she couldn't see why gentlemen would find any particular attraction in her niece's calm, classical features and plain fair hair. Beside the golden Annabella, Mary would fade into insignificance. Lady Winter's strongest motherly trait, besides an understandable matchmaking urge, was a firm belief in her daughter's superior physical attributes. She couldn't fathom why Annabella wouldn't want to exploit Mary as a foil for her own beauty.

"You know, miss, I'm bringing the girl into public this winter with you, like it or not," she stated.

"But Mama!"

"No buts. What have you against her? Afraid she'll steal your beaux?"

Annabella let out a trill of laughter. "If dear Mary doesn't want to go into society, as I know she does not, you will force her?" Her blue eyes were full of sympathy.

"Demmed right I'd force her," said Lady Winter. "D'you think I want the girl on my hands for life? Come to think of it, I may not have the magic touch when it comes to firing off young ladies. I didn't get rid of you in your first season."

"Mama," Annabella whined, "if you'd spent more on my wardrobe, if we could have lived in town instead of out here in the wilds, if we'd got into Almack's..." One of her most sensitive points was the fact that she hadn't been snapped up the instant she'd appeared in town the previous spring. She was convinced that if her parents really cared for her chances, they would have rented a house in Mayfair and not thrust her into a carriage for the tedious drive from Woodbank Hall for every social occasion.

Lady Winter declined to make any answer to her daughter's charges, concentrating instead on running a brush through Mack's unruly coat. It was at this uncomfortable moment that Mary happened to walk into the morning room.

Annabella glared at her cousin, which led Mary to suppose that she had interrupted a sensitive scene. With murmured apologies, she began to back out of the room.

"Hold on there, miss." Her aunt stopped her with an imperious raised hand. "Your presence is wanted here; come and sit. I've just been telling Annabella that we're all going to make a shopping excursion into London. To buy you a new dress for the hunt ball."

Annabella sighed audibly; this had been the unhappy result of trying to direct her mama's thinking. She had hoped to gain her mother's support by her expression of concern for her cousin's comfort. The fact that Mary had nothing suitable to wear had seemed assured to elicit her mother's agreement. Annabella had then planned that this information should lead up to a tale of Mary's selfishness with her possessions, which Mama would in turn follow with a lecture to Mary and the insistence that Mary lend her garnet necklace to the deserving Annabella.

"I couldn't let you do that, ma'am," Mary said demurely, willing herself not to smile at her cousin's black looks.

"No argument! Annabella tells me you're not wanting to go into public, and that shyness must be nipped in the bud if you're to make a suitable match.

It's settled. The three of us are going into town to-morrow.''

Mary opened her mouth and shut it again, deciding not to protest that she had never confided anything to Annabella, let alone a supposed shyness.

''Someday, ma'am, I'll pay you back for all your kindness,'' she said instead, with her brightest smile.

Lady Winter met her eyes and grinned in return. ''Something tells me, my dear, you'll appear to advantage once we get you out of those mourning rags. My daughter will have to look sharp!''

Annabella, her rather wide mouth set in a tight line, flounced out of the room.

''She needs it,'' Aunt Winter said airily when Mary, a touch disingenuously, apologized for causing her cousin pain.

Mary had to agree, silently, that a disappointment or two would do her cousin Annabella a world of good.

THE NEXT MORNING, a crisp day under a grey November sky, the three ladies stepped up into the Winters' smart chaise. Lady Winter was as particular about her vehicles as she was about the cattle that drew them, and she nodded in approval at the coachman and the footmen who were to ride along, acknowledging their sparkling liveries as well as the spotless state of the coach.

Lady Winter was attired in her best for this visit to London, in a claret-coloured walking ensemble and a smart bonnet. She looked every inch the lady, and not at all the sort of woman who was wont to spend most days with her apparel in a horrifying state of mud and stable straw and dog hair. Annabella outshone her mother in a lovely russet pelisse with a capelet of soft brown fur, which also trimmed her fashionably high-crowned velvet bonnet. Mary felt more out of place than usual in her plain walking things: a grey wrapping-coat and her best black gown, set off by a straw bonnet with grey ribbons. At least, she reflected, the drapers and dressmakers would know her on sight for a young woman in desperate need of clothes.

"Do you like my new walking dress, Cousin?" Annabella asked in a cheerful voice, landing rather heavily on the squabs. "It cost the earth."

The ten miles to town passed pleasantly enough. The well-sprung carriage drawn by Lady Winter's prize team of blacks bowled effortlessly down the lanes near home and then onto the turnpike road. Lady Winter immediately indulged in her favourite pursuit during a carriage ride; her eyes closed, and now and then she emitted a robust snore. Mary, sitting with her back to the horses, looked out of the window and tried to ignore Annabella's cattish comments on this and that lady, many of whom Mary had never met. It was amazing what a number of females lived only to try to get back at Annabella for stealing their beaux.

At length, the necessary slowing of the vehicle as they neared Hyde Park Corner jostled Lady Winter awake. She looked about her, blinking. "Here already, are we? Well, young ladies, there is something I must tell you—"

She was interrupted when the carriage slowed to a halt by the side of the Knightsbridge Road. The first footman's head appeared at the window, and he called out, "Hyde Park Corner, milady. You wished to be informed."

Lady Winter cleared her throat. "Now, you girls will be on your own for the next little while." Fishing in her reticule, she came up with a purse which she pressed into Annabella's hands. "There's enough to frank you for the next couple of hours at whatever place we don't have credit, though if you mention your papa's name, Annabella, anyone should take your custom and send the reckoning to Woodbank Hall."

"You're leaving us to shop alone, Aunt?" Mary asked in dismay. She hadn't counted on a day spent tête-à-tête with Annabella.

Her cousin's eyes had begun to gleam as she stashed the purse away in her own reticule. "Where will you be, Mama?"

Lady Winter said, "There's a very fine auction hard by here, my dears, and some items I wish to look at. You'd be bored silly, and then you know we have only the day to find a gown for Mary, so you must go along to the shops at a good clip."

"What sort of items, Aunt?"

"Not some bankrupt's household effects, Mama," cried Annabella. "You really ought not to be seen at such a place."

Lady Winter looked the picture of guilt as she denied any intention of going to see some poor devil's goods put on the block.

"I know what it is," said Annabella in triumph. "You mean to go to Tattersall's again, Mama, and you know how Papa feels about it. No lady..."

As Annabella's tirade went on, Mary's eyes widened. By Aunt Winter's vexed expression, she surmised that Annabella was on the mark. And even Mary, with her lack of town bronze, knew that ladies did not commonly set foot in Tattersall's, the famous Horse Repository. It would hardly be worse for Lady Winter to stride into White's and sit down to play whist or dine.

"I shall have no choice but to tell Papa." Annabella finished her speech on a note of self-righteousness, but Mary noticed that a shrewd gleam had appeared in her cousin's eye. "Unless, Mama, you choose to make me a very pretty present. A new gown, say, for the ball?"

Lady Winter frowned. "My girl, you've had at least two new ball gowns ready and waiting this past month."

"A whole month! They must be woefully out of fashion." Annabella's voice was smooth, reasonable. Mary had the feeling she was watching a mistress of manipulation at work.

"I won't pay for your silence, you snippy thing," said Lady Winter. Mary had halfway expected her to turn conciliatory, to wheedle her daughter into keeping quiet, but she did nothing of the sort, and her niece felt like applauding. "I'll tell Sir Egbert myself what I've done when we get home tonight. I don't expect you to understand, Annabella, but there is a rare prize hunter coming on the block today, one of Lord Frederick Reardon's stallions out of Morning Star, and I daren't miss my chance. And I must go with only one of the footmen, for you're right, my dear, *young* ladies mustn't be seen in Tatt's. Your reputations wouldn't be worth a groat. You may take the second footman, and I'll collect you in Layton and Shears' in two hours. Is that clear?"

The two young ladies sat silent in response to this torrent of words.

"And," her ladyship added with a shrewd glance at her daughter, "you are to buy today, miss, a dress-length for a new morning gown, a pair of slippers, evening gloves, stockings, and a fan. Not a thread more, do you hear? I'm not franking you for a new ball gown when you've dresses at home that ain't been seen once."

Annabella sighed. "Oh, Mama."

During this conversation the Winter carriage had remained stationary at the edge of the Knightsbridge Road. The footman who had been waiting outside the carriage door stretched up to say, "Milady, the steps?"

Mary giggled. Only his forehead, wrinkled from the strain, and his slightly bulging eyes were visible above the glass. Lady Winter gave her permission with a curt syllable, and the footman flung open the door and placed the steps.

"Thank you, Paul," said Lady Winter. "You girls behave yourselves. You are to go straight to Oxford Street, mind. Coachman has his instructions, and James is to stay by you at all times."

"Yes, Mama," said Annabella in an uncharacteristically meek voice.

"Have a good time, Aunt," Mary added, her own voice doubtful. She was still a little shocked at Aunt

Winter's plan, but that feeling was nearly sunk in her admiration of her ladyship's steadfastness in standing up to her sly daughter.

Lady Winter nodded briskly, beckoned to the footman, and marched away down the street while Mary watched out the window.

"Shall we be going?" Annabella said loudly, speaking out of the opposite window. "Oxford Street, Coachman."

The equipage began to move and was soon trotting, as smartly as traffic would allow, up Piccadilly.

Mary had only been to London on one or two occasions, and never to shop. She was becoming excited in spite of all fears of what a day with Annabella would be like. She stared out at the streets, entranced by the numbers of fashionable people, street vendors, shabby citizens and military men. London, the fascinating town, the capital of the world according to all the British soldiers Mary had known in her time. She was finally going to get to know this great city which was part of her heritage.

Mary reached into her reticule to finger the cheap binding of the book she had placed there. *The Picture of London*, the 1802 edition. The little book was covered in red and had been a gift from Papa on Mary's twelfth birthday, an odd souvenir of a homeland she had rarely seen. She had been longing to explore London ever since.

She knew very well that this day would bring not adventure, but a new gown. She withdrew her hand from her reticule. Perhaps some other day Papa would bring her into London for sightseeing. She doubted it, but there was more sense in hoping for Papa to oblige her than in asking Annabella to forego her shopping for a tour of the Tower or Saint Paul's.

The coach rattled into Oxford Street. Within two minutes Annabella was pulling the check-string.

"We might as well get out here and walk along to the draper's," she said, giving Mary's costume the only critical look she had bothered to bestow that morning. "You *are* just back from the Peninsula. That ought to excuse your clothes."

"Thanks, coz," Mary said, shaking her head as she followed Annabella's sumptuously clad form out of the carriage and onto the pavement.

The procession was soon organized. James, a lanky young man somewhat too long for his livery, was detailed to follow discreetly behind the young ladies, and Coachman told to meet them at a certain glover's in the space of one hour. They would then see where they should go before the scheduled rendezvous point at Layton and Shears'. Annabella, with her vast experience of the London shops, led the way down the street when the carriage had departed, leaving Mary and James to scramble after her as best they could.

The first stop was a *plumassier*, where Annabella bought some ostrich plumes and four red silk flowers despite Mary's one ventured comment that perhaps bloodred was not her cousin's best colour, given the ruddy cast of her hair.

"Pooh! What do you know?" was Annabella's rejoinder, uttered in a merry voice that removed much of its sting. Annabella was in her shopping mode now, and nothing could distress her.

The next merchant to receive their custom was a milliner. Annabella demanded that Mary be the one to choose between a cottage bonnet of robin's-egg silk and satin straw or a green velvet wide-brimmed hat lined with white lace.

"They are both delightful, Cousin," Mary was beginning, intending to add that Annabella's mama didn't expect her to buy bonnets, when Annabella forestalled her by telling the shop assistant that her cousin was correct, of course she must have both creations.

James's burdens were growing by the minute, but Mary noticed that she was no closer to a new dress than she'd been when she got up that morning. She followed Annabella out of the milliner's, heading for the draper's at last, or so Annabella claimed.

The cold air, after the stuffy atmosphere of the hat shop, revived Mary, and she was about to step up to Annabella's side rather than trail behind her when that young lady stopped abruptly in her tracks, nearly causing Mary to bump into her.

"Corinna!" cried Annabella with a little squeal, and she cast herself into the arms of a fashionable young lady who had been walking in the other direction and now returned the embrace with an answering cry.

Mary and an indulgent middle-aged maid who apparently belonged to the young woman addressed as Corinna looked on at the reunion.

"Dear Annabella, it's been months!"

"Heavens, are you wintering in town, my dear? Only fancy, my parents still have me rusticating in the country."

"Can you come along and drink tea at my mother's?"

"I fear not, I have to meet Mama in a short time."

The other young lady's raven curls and large, dark blue eyes gave her the look of a pleasant person. Her smile was friendly, and her clothes were elegance itself without a touch of the overdone—unlike Annabella's. Mary stood by expectantly, anxious to meet this paragon.

At last Corinna, feeling Mary's eyes upon her, turned to see who was regarding her.

Annabella was recalled to her surroundings. Her eyes shifted from Mary to her friend and back again. Shoving her gloved hands even deeper into her large fur muff, she laughed lightly. "Don't stare so, Mary, even if you do come from the country. Help James with the packages, there's a good girl."

Mary stood still, the shock of what had just happened holding her motionless.

"Don't dawdle, girl, you heard your mistress," added Corinna, and, linking her arm through Annabella's, she turned to retrace her steps, saying that she was so glad to see her dear friend that she would conduct her personally to her next stop, never mind the time.

Annabella gave Mary a crooked little smile and a shrug, then turned her attention entirely to her friend. Corinna's maid stepped to Mary's side.

"This is beyond anything," Mary heard herself saying. Both girls turned back, Corinna's face betraying her displeasure at a servant's insubordination, Annabella's a study in awe, stubbornness and guilt. Corinna's servant gasped. Mary knew that James, standing behind her, had witnessed the whole thing and would spread it throughout Woodbank Hall by nightfall that Miss Annabella had given a rare setdown to that foreign miss.

"Good day to you, *Cousin* Annabella," Mary said, turning on her heel. Without looking back, she marched down the street. She didn't expect anyone to follow her, and, sure enough, no one did.

Mary held her head high, a little smile curving her lips as she mentally compared Annabella's expression to that of a fish, a startled deer, a guilty little girl. Her step was light as she proceeded down the street. She hardly noticed the people around her and was careful, even in her odd mood, not to meet any gentlemen's eyes. She hadn't felt so free since she had come to live in England.

CHAPTER FOUR

"IMPOSSIBLE! I CAN'T BE LOST," Mary was muttering some twenty minutes later. She frowned at the buildings all about her and buried her nose for the fourteenth time in *The Picture of London*. She had no idea where she was, and she more than suspected that she had been going in circles.

In the last little while she had asked directions of four street urchins and a haughty lady's maid who had acted as though Mary were begging for alms. Everyone she had asked pointed the young woman confidently toward Hyde Park Corner, where Mary believed Tattersall's was located. Her only difficulty lay in the fact that not all of the opinions she had solicited coincided with one another. As a result, Mary was standing in a narrow street near what looked to be the back entrance of a fine mansion—quite probably no nearer to Tattersall's and her aunt's protection than when she had turned her back on Annabella and company in Oxford Street.

Exhilarating though it was to stride about the town alone, Mary knew that she had to go to her aunt, and at once. It was either that or crawl after Annabella and her detestable friend, for Mary had no illusions that she, a stranger to London without enough pocket money to hire a hackney, could return to Woodbank Hall in the independent style she would have preferred.

She had decided instead to go to Tattersall's as quickly as possible, tell Aunt Winter that she had lost Annabella and the footman, and leave it at that. She wouldn't bear tales of Annabella's silly and hurtful behaviour, tempting though that prospect was. She would maintain her dignity in the face of her aunt's probing questions.

There would be no chance to display such a noble demeanour, though, unless she could find Lady Winter in the first place. Mary sighed, wishing her guidebook weren't ten years old and that she had called upon more knowledgeable people to direct her. Glancing about, she noticed a porter lounging near the back gate of the grand house in front of her. She started toward him. There wasn't another creature in sight, save for a small boy wheeling a covered barrow, and Mary was disenchanted with the navigational talents of small boys.

"Well, my pretty," said a voice from behind her shoulder, "are you touring London?"

Mary wheeled round; a large man seemed to have appeared from out of nowhere. His wide mouth was set in a leer, and a pair of small grey eyes glittered down. He was fairly young and very burly. The elegant fabric of the coat and trousers stretched on his massive frame suggested a gentleman. His voice, however, betrayed something which Mary knew put him in a class beneath her own. His social standing aside, instinct told her this was no chivalrous soul bent on helping a lady in distress. How could she get away?

Thinking quickly, she made a slight curtsey as if in greeting. The man did indeed pause in his menacing approach, consternation at her courteous behaviour clear in his face, and Mary ducked past him in a sudden lunge.

Unfortunately, the man reached out a long arm and captured her round the waist, the whole operation apparently effortless and taking less than a second. "Here, there's no need to be in a hurry, ma'am. If it's London life you've a mind to see, there's no better guide than your friend Tom Trumble."

Mary struggled, cursing herself for carrying the guidebook in her hands. She ought to have known it would mark her as a green miss if anyone recognized it.

The man identified as Trumble crushed Mary in his arms and attempted to snatch a kiss. Mary did not hesitate. She turned her face to one side, squeezed her eyes shut, muttered a short Spanish phrase of prayer, and brought her knee up in a sharp gesture taught her by Doña Luisa, her old duenna. She had never before had occasion to defend herself in this way. She could only hope that the prayer would be answered as Doña Luisa had promised.

It was. Trumble emitted a startled yelp and dropped his prey. Mary fell to the pavement, catching herself awkwardly with one arm. Her backside connected with the hard surface, and she let out a startled little "Oof!"

Her attacker had also dropped to the ground, she noticed in surprise. Surely she had not hit him that hard. He was clutching himself oddly, but his face looked not so much pained as angry. Mary inched away, struggling to stand up.

The man reached out and grasped one of her ankles. "Not so fast, my dear," he snarled in a voice laden with anger. "We've unfinished business."

"Sir, let me go," said Mary. Somewhere in the back of her mind she realized that calmness, reasoning with the man, was her only chance. She wished her instinct hadn't led her to bring her knee up; she must hope he would overlook that liberty. Glancing over her shoulder as she tried desperately to pull her ankle free and only strained it in the process, she wondered what on earth the stupid porter of the elegant house could be thinking of not to interfere. He must still be at his post. Was London so corrupt and sophisticated a place that an able-bodied man could watch another attack an innocent woman?

Mary had no time to ponder this question. Tom Trumble was pulling her closer to him by means of her poor ankle. With the other foot, she kicked out again.

"No, you don't," her captor snarled out. He released her leg and made as if to grab her waist or shoulders.

Somehow Mary managed to roll away and stagger to her feet. She wasted no words on the dreadful stranger; she merely took off running, relieved to find that her ankle wasn't in as bad a case as she had feared.

To her horror, a strong hand seized her arm, bringing her to a stop. Confused—for she knew Trumble to be still on the ground—Mary looked up into a pair of liquid dark eyes.

"We meet again, *señorita,*" said a raven-haired young man. "Is this creature—" he nodded disdainfully at the large Trumble, who was just getting to his feet "—being less than gallant?"

"Yes," Mary was able to whisper through her shock. Facing her was the young man who had helped her with papa on the night of the Hollands' party, the young man she had dared to dream about.

They were speaking in Spanish. "Frenchies!" exclaimed Tom Trumble, advancing with a menacing tread. "Spies, are you? Adds a bit of colour to my fun."

Something flashed. The man Trumble let out a yelp, and Mary, suddenly blushing, turned her head away from the sight of her erstwhile attacker. His loosely cut trousers, relieved of their side buttons, were bunched about his ankles. Mercifully, his shirt was long enough to cover what was best left unobserved by maiden eyes. He was staring down at himself, blinking in surprise, his mouth agape.

The Spanish gentleman, smiling, sheathed his duelling foil. He had brought it out so quickly that an ill-timed blink would have robbed the observer of the amusing sight of his sword point nicking off first one, then the other of Tom Trumble's trouser buttons.

Mary, her gaze still modestly averted, wondered why on earth the young Spaniard was carrying a sword. No one did these days, except on ceremonial occasions, and her saviour was dressed in an ordinary morning costume of buff pantaloons and blue coat, not a formal court dress studded with diplomatic orders such as he had sported in Mary's daydreams.

"Shall we leave this gentleman to his toilette?" whispered that deep, thrilling voice into Mary's ear. "It would be best to see you on to your destination, true?"

She nodded. She couldn't help glancing back, just once, at her vanquished tormentor. An awful scowl on his face, Tom Trumble was adjusting his trousers round his waist as he stared, puzzled, at a large brass button in one hand. Mary giggled.

The Spaniard took her arm and whisked her out of sight of Trumble, around the corner. Only when they had emerged onto a bustling, fashionable thoroughfare did he slow his pace.

"Thank you so much, sir," Mary said in heartfelt gratitude. "This is the second time you've come to my aid. Where did you appear from so suddenly?"

He smiled into her eyes. "I thank God I was at hand, *señorita*. I was leaving my establishment in the Albany when I saw you struggling with that monster. I recognized you, of course."

Of course? Mary felt her cheeks grow hot. It was not a matter of course for her to be noticed and remembered by gentlemen. On the contrary, it was a delightful novelty.

"I've been wishing that I could have thanked you properly for the help you gave my father that night," she said shyly, "and now I have another favour to be grateful for. You won't disappear again, will you, before I can give you my thanks?''

"I believe you already did that, *señorita,* and rest assured that I'll stay by you until I see you safe with your duenna. Where are you going?''

"Tattersall's,'' said Mary without thinking. The young man, being Spanish, had naturally thought that Mary must have strayed from the side of a chaperone. If he only knew that she had willfully marched away from her only London acquaintance!

The gentleman's face betrayed his shock, and Mary remembered too late what a terrible place Tattersall's horse auction was supposed to be for young ladies. There was no help for it; Tattersall's was where she was going. Quickly she explained that her aunt was there, and that having been separated from her cousin by accident, she was headed for the one place where she knew she had a duenna.

"Most wise of you, *señorita,*'' answered her escort. "Tell me—we have gone through adversity together twice now—would it be proper for us to introduce ourselves?''

Mary had been wishing for some time that she could find out this kind stranger's name. "I am Mary Winter. And you, sir?''

"Antonio Ramirez y Mondego,'' said the young man with a sweeping bow that angled his sword point out into the air. An elegant dandy, just passing by, scurried away with a horrified look.

Mary had to laugh. "And your sword? Do you carry such a thing in case you come upon young women in need of rescue?''

"Ah, no. I am a master of fencing by profession, Miss Winter. I have a studio in the Albany. I try, in my modest way, to fill the gap left by the great Mr. Angelo, who used to have his establishment there. Here, *señorita*. The front entrance of my abode. A handsome little house for a town, don't you agree?"

Mary looked at the building he had indicated. They were just passing by. "Shops?" she said in confusion. She had heard that the Albany was a magnificent town house once owned by a noble family until it had been given over to gentlemen's apartments. At first glance there was no town palace, only a row of very handsome commercial establishments, with decorative columns evenly spaced and brass eagles supporting first-floor balconies above the shop windows.

Ramirez explained that the shops were merely a façade and directed her attention to the magnificent front of the main house, visible behind a central gate. "Such an original English idea, splitting up a noble residence into rooms. I delight in living here."

"And working, too? Do you enjoy your fencing instruction?"

"The sword is an art which is esteemed by many gentlemen. I have a skill that way, as it happens. It fetches me a good living."

"Then you're not—you don't work for. . ." Mary's voice trailed away. When she had seen this man at Holland House she had immediately guessed him to be a diplomat, someone of importance in the Spanish government. Never would she have set him down as a mere fencing master.

"I work for myself, ma'am," said Ramirez smoothly. He smiled down at Mary, and there was an understanding in his eyes which made her feel ashamed of letting her surprise show. She longed to tell him that she thought no less of him for earning his living, that she had merely believed him so magnificent that he must be an ambassador at the least.

"And have you been in England long?" she confined herself to asking, though she knew that even such a mild question might betray her unseemly interest in this near-stranger. Resolutely she told herself that she was simply making conversation and that nobody would read more than mere politeness into her query.

"A few years. My parents died shortly before Bonaparte's troops first came to Spain under the guise of helping to keep the peace. Our estates were impoverished, and I thought it best to leave my country for a time, to improve my lot and study how to stand up to the invader."

"Oh! And what have you learned?"

"That the defense of Spain is a complicated matter, *señorita,* and that our struggle will not be won in a day," he answered.

Mary nodded, struck by the intensity of his words. She waited for the inevitable questions about herself and her background, and when they didn't come she was conscious of a nagging feeling of irritation. Wasn't he at all curious about who she was, where she came from?

Ramirez didn't appear to note the flash of displeasure which crossed Mary's face. His moment of seriousness over, he became the knowledgeable guide to London's sights, telling Mary that they were presently walking down Piccadilly, pointing out this and that sight as they made their way through the press of shoppers and strollers. Mary's hand rested in the crook of Ramirez's arm. She forgot her moment of pique and began to enjoy herself wholeheartedly. Here she was in London on a fine, if grey, day, walking down a famous thoroughfare with a handsome, well-dressed man. She had nothing to wish for but a less shabby outfit.

Green Park was at their left, Ramirez informed her, but they didn't cross the road. "It would be best," the young man explained stiffly, "if a young lady did not walk in the park with a gentleman not her brother."

"How very Spanish you are, *señor*," Mary responded with a little smile and a secret, sinking feeling. He couldn't have any respect for her, a female he had found wandering about on her own, open to lewd invitations from any and all molesters, and whom he was now conducting to Tattersall's, but he maintained a fair imitation of it as the walk went on.

Soon, having crossed a street and dodged the innumerable carriages and equestrians in the bustle of Hyde Park Turnpike, Mary and her escort stood before the entrance of a huge, hulking building. "The famous Tattersall's, *señorita*. Shall we enter?"

Mary gave a brave nod. In two minutes she would be with Aunt Winter, she reminded herself. She was safe now.

They walked into a spacious courtyard. Sounds assailed Mary's ears: the neighing of horses and the deep or strident voices of men. A crowd of gentlemen stood or walked about, all sorts of men, from carefully dressed gentlemen of ton to coarsely garbed individuals. Beyond the forest of men one could see shining carriages ranged along the walls on display. The occasional horse paraded through, led by a trainer. In the centre of the courtyard was placed a high, ornamental cupola surmounted by a bust which Ramirez whispered was of the Prince Regent.

Mary instinctively clung tighter to her new friend's arm. "I must find my aunt," she murmured as one masculine face after another paused in talk or promenade to stare incredulously at her. "Do you see any women, *señor?* She's bound to be the only one here."

Ramirez opened his mouth to answer; at that moment clutching hands appeared behind him and grabbed. Mary gasped. Tom Trumble had followed them.

"Shame me in public, will you, Frenchie spy?" the burly man snarled. Mary noticed, even through her horror, that Trumble's trousers were awkwardly fastened with pins. He threw Mary's saviour to the ground as he spoke and was proceeding to throttle him. Ramirez, caught by surprise, didn't look to be holding his own. His duelling foil clinked uselessly beside him as his gloved hands came up to clasp Tom Trumble by his thick neck.

Mary didn't pause to think. The unfairness of the encounter moved her to action. Dark eyes flashing, she marched over to the pair and aimed a kick at Trumble's posterior. The two men rolled as her foot shot out, her long skirt gave a loud sound of protest as it ripped loose from her bodice, and she was thrown to the ground. She knocked her head on the stones and was momentarily stunned, only dimly aware of the battle going on beside her and the spectators who were gathering, with excited shouts and jostlings, in a ring around the strange trio. Mary heard a truly sickening crunch, and she shut her eyes. She knew that Ramirez had been badly hurt.

Then comforting arms closed around her, and she opened her eyes. Ramirez! "You're all right," she said softly. "He didn't—"

"No," answered the other, "I did." He signalled over his shoulder, and Mary peeked from the safe shelter of his embrace to see Trumble, unconscious on the ground, the apparent victim of a solid right to the jaw.

"Oh." She sighed in relief, nestling even closer.

"Well, missy," said a crisp, familiar voice, "I'll delight to hear your explanation of this."

A strange feeling assailed Mary's senses as she stared up into the face of Letitia Winter.

CHAPTER FIVE

IN AN INSTANT Mary came back to reality. No longer
was she the captive princess delivered from danger,
clinging to the bold knight who had ridden to her rescue. She was only a reckless girl who had some explaining to do.

Thinking she heard a soft, masculine chuckle near
her ear, Mary glared into the eyes of Ramirez for one
instant and then disengaged herself from his arms.
How provoking that he should see humour in this
predicament, for she had a nearly overwhelming desire to laugh herself, a feeling she was determined not
to give in to, and Ramirez was not helping. Aunt
Winter would surely look askance at a niece who not
only took part in masculine altercations at Tattersall's but thought them a laughing matter. Mary rose
as gracefully as she could, brushing off the assistance
of Ramirez, and faced her aunt.

Lady Winter's expression was a wonder to behold.
Her strong features registered disbelief as her gaze
roved over her dishevelled young relation.

"My dear girl, you've torn it this time," she said,
shaking her head.

Mary looked down at her ripped gown and hastily
rewrapped her loose pelisse, wishing the outer gar-

ment had buttons. Inexpert though she was at slang expressions, she realized even as she covered herself that her aunt's words referred not to her regrettable state of dress, but to the situation in which she found herself.

"I—I did not intend this to happen," she began lamely.

"Niece, I would hate to see something you had planned, if this is an example of your impromptu activity," returned Aunt Winter at her most imperious. Indeed she looked almost regal in her uncommonly fine walking costume; that she was surrounded by wealthy-looking gentlemen seemed her due, though the gentlemen in question were occupied to a man in staring at the lady's niece. Mary instinctively drew her pelisse even tighter about her ruined gown and stepped an inch closer to Ramirez.

"Young man," snapped Lady Winter, fixing her eyes on the dark-haired individual who had been found molesting her niece. "You, I trust, will have no objection to appearing before the magistrate for this heinous crime."

Mary gasped. The ever-growing circle of gentlemen pressed closer, and one or two deep voices even offered to seize her rescuer. "This is ridiculous," she cried. "*Señor*—that is, Mr. Ramirez saved me from that horrid man on the floor. *He*—" and she pointed an accusing finger at the unconscious heap that was Tom Trumble "—tried to attack me in the street, and when Mr. Ramirez chastised him the wretch followed us here and set upon him. By all means have someone cart that fiend off to the magistrate."

Mary had a fine, clear voice, and by the end of her speech she would not have appeared to disadvantage upon the boards. A young buck standing near Lady Winter clapped his gloved hands together and burst out, "Very fine. Well said, ma'am."

At that moment one of the managers rushed up, demanding to be told why his exclusive establishment had suddenly staged a scene more suited to Cribb's Parlour. A babbel of male voices rushed to answer, and Lady Winter took the opportunity to advance upon Mary and her rescuer, grasp each young culprit by an elbow, and propel the pair to a secluded corner of the courtyard behind a shiny landau.

"Well, miss, you've managed to make a mull of it for sure. And after all my hopes for you!" was Aunt Winter's opening statement once they had reached this relative sanctuary.

"Hopes? For me?" Mary's voice as well as her face reflected her puzzlement.

"Yes, widgeon, that you'd make a good match this season and be one up on that foolish daughter of mine. Now you've gone and ruined yourself before most of the men who count in society. What am I to do with you but seclude you at Woodbank Hall, which is what Annabella wanted all along?"

Mary could only stare at her aunt as these words sank in. They made little sense to her logical mind. She, to have made a good match in society? Impossible. She had a connection or two, but hampered by her Spanish blood and her total lack of dowry, not to mention her quiet looks, she hadn't expected to do more than hug the wall at whatever social events she would be permitted to attend.

"By the way," her aunt was continuing, "what *have* you done with Annabella?"

Mary recited her story of having lost Annabella and the footman in Oxford Street—accidentally, of course. She felt more than a little virtuous as she neglected to mention her cousin's shabby treatment of her.

"As you see, Madam, the young lady only came to this place because it was the sole choice she had," Ramirez put in with a bow. A little frown drawing his eyebrows together, he added, "Though it would seem Madam must be an extraordinary lady indeed, not to have her own spotless reputation harmed by a visit to this masculine stronghold."

"Er, as you say," responded Lady Winter with a cough and an even steelier glance. "Whether my niece meant harm or not is really outside of the question. She's ruined, as sure as if she'd danced naked in Carlton House."

Mary writhed at these words. It was true enough that she had unintentionally put herself beyond the pale, but such language! Would she ever get used to Aunt Winter?

"I beg to differ, Madam," said Ramirez. "May not a young lady's intended save her from an attacker? After such a scare, may she not rest in the arms of her husband-to-be without losing her fame? It is unfortunate that this happened in Tattersall's, but it was not Miss Winter's fault. She had to come to you, and you were here, my lady. You cannot blame her for that."

"What in heaven's name are you saying?" cried Mary. Intended, indeed! He couldn't mean . . .

"Young man," Mary's aunt said at the same time, "my niece is to have no fortune."

"Fortune! What is that?" Ramirez tossed off this problem with a wave of his gloved hand, slightly bloodied by an encounter with Tom Trumble's nose. "She is of a noble Spanish family. And as for the English side, it is for you to inform *me* if there is anything amiss."

"The Winters," said Lady Winter in a chilling tone, "are of the utmost respectability. *I* condescended to marry into them."

"Ah! Your pardon, Madam. Who could wish for further proof than that?" Ramirez replied smoothly.

"Wait," said Mary. "How do you know my Spanish family, sir? And what are the two of you saying? You can't—you mustn't . . ." Her voice trailed off; she couldn't continue. There would be nothing worse than to protest a marriage proposal, only to find that the two others were discussing something else altogether.

Yet what else but marriage could it be? She must assert herself, must fight to see that her life wasn't disposed of in this cold, high-handed manner. She had always detested the thought of a marriage of convenience.

"As for you, young man," said Aunt Winter, giving Mary only one finger lifted in warning to prove she had heard the girl, "what are your prospects? You're a foreigner, I perceive."

"He is a fencing master," Mary informed her aunt. She didn't know whether she was trying to shock Lady

Winter or embarrass Ramirez by this revelation. She might have added that he was admitted socially to the highest diplomatic circles, but she did not. Ramirez looked at her curiously, and she lowered her eyes. She had just said something which could be interpreted as snobbery, and she stubbornly refused to rectify the impression.

"A fencing master of the highest repute," Ramirez added with a suave smile, "as many of the men here would be happy to attest."

"But a fencing—a master of any kind—" Aunt Winter was spluttering when Ramirez interrupted.

"And Count Antonio Ramirez y Mondego, of Castile." He hesitated and smiled at Mary, whose mouth had dropped open upon hearing that she had been walking and talking with a Spanish nobleman. "Lord Holland can confirm that I am who I say I am, if you care to send a message to him."

"Oh." Lady Winter gave the young man a hard look. "My niece is a countrywoman of yours on her mother's side."

"Aunt!" exclaimed Mary. Her momentary fascination with Ramirez's rank was over. "I will not be palmed off in this manner. I insist—"

"You, my girl, have forfeited the right to insist on anything. This gentleman is being good enough to offer to repair the damage, so to speak. It is my duty in this situation to act for your father, who heaven knows isn't even out of bed yet, so we can't expect him to give consent."

"Nobody has to give consent," snapped Mary. "I'm twenty-two."

"There is that." Lady Winter nodded soberly, then turned to Ramirez. "She ain't exactly in her first season, you know, young man."

"Such perfection could not have been attained in less than two-and-twenty years," was Ramirez's smooth reply.

"Fustian," said Mary. "Flattery, sir, will get you nowhere. My aunt has told you I'm not wealthy, but penniless in fact, and now we've added a delicate allusion to my years. And I have no desire to be married off, scandal or no scandal. I can live as an independent woman, a teacher or companion. But not the wife of a—a—"

"Pity," said Ramirez, "you seemed to like me well enough before I expressed a desire to marry you."

Mary looked away. There was something too knowing about this man. Did he guess that she was more than a little attracted to him? That would be fatal, for her attraction did not alter her resolve to choose her own mate, when and where she would. This was not the dark ages, nor was it Spain.

"Arranged marriages are still the accepted thing in my country, Madam," Ramirez was saying to Lady Winter. He might have been reading Mary's thoughts. "No doubt Inez de la Rosa would have been happy to see her daughter become the countess of such an ancient family—fallen upon hard times, alas, which is why you see me carrying this sword."

"Ridiculous," said Mary. Once again she wondered how in the world he knew who her mother had been. She didn't remember telling him during their walk, but she supposed she might have done. She had been a trifle flustered in his company.

Lady Winter beckoned one of her gentleman friends. Many of the men were clustering close to what was now the centre of the drama; for the manager of Tattersall's had had the inert form of Tom Trumble taken away, draped across the back of a blood stallion.

"Stephens, this gentleman is my niece's betrothed. They have kept their attachment a secret from me, and now I must make certain he is a suitable match. Run along to Kensington and ask Lord Holland—" Lady Winter hesitated, glancing at Ramirez in consternation. Mary could see her difficulty; if Ramirez turned out to be as respectable, nay, noble as he said he was, there was no point in insulting him now.

Mary had no such compunction. "Ask him if this gentleman is an imposter," she said clearly.

Ramirez directed a smile at Lady Winter, whose face registered her shock at Mary's lack of tact. "Perhaps this card will aid your friend in his interrogation," he said, putting an engraved piece of pasteboard into the lady's hand.

Stephens, a large, rawboned sporting sort in late middle age, lumbered off, and Lady Winter looked about her at the other gentlemen. She next extracted a visiting card of her own from her reticule, fished out a pencil, and scribbled a note on the back. "You, Lord Cathcott." She singled out a slender young man in the extravagant uniform of a tulip of the ton. "The Bishop's your mother's relation, is he not? Take him this with my compliments."

"But, Madam," protested the young man. "Walk in on the Bishop? Don't know him well, that is to say, don't know if—"

Lady Winter tossed off these shrill bleatings with a wave of her hand. "My family is well known to His Lordship, and he should be charmed to do me a small favour. What's one special license more or less? Oh, and take him this." Lastly she withdrew a fat purse from the reticule and passed it to the astonished Cathcott. The youthful peer ducked his head and obediently set out.

"Aunt, I must protest," cried Mary. "I won't wed this gentleman. Why disturb the Bishop?"

Lady Winter took another glance round at the company. "Dear girl, what manners! Naturally you wish to wed your own fiancé."

Mary remembered that the major feature of her aunt's plan was the fiction of an engagement between herself and Ramirez. She sighed.

"Let's not air the family linen in public," Lady Winter went on. "We'll adjourn to the Red Lion. And you—" Once more she pointed her finger, this time at a quiet, scholarly-looking man Mary was later to learn was a duke "—tell Stephens and Cathcott where to find us."

"A splendid idea, Madam. Privacy is wanted," Ramirez put in, and to Mary's disgust he offered an arm to each of the two ladies. Followed at a distance by Paul, the Winters' first footman, the trio marched out of Tattersall's. Mary's dignity was slightly hampered by the ripped skirt which hung down over her feet in front and caused her to trip more than once.

Though she did try, she wasn't able both to hold the skirt up and clutch her pelisse closed to hide its ripped front, and she knew the latter was the more important chore.

Because she didn't know what else to do, Mary walked calmly enough beside Ramirez. Both young people matched their strides to the energetic pace of Lady Winter. In this manner they promenaded across Green Park and then up Pall Mall, never slackening their pace until they reached a small way labelled Crown Passage. Her hearty ladyship described the Red Lion as "only a step away," but it seemed a long enough walk to Mary, who was imprisoned not only by her ruined ensemble but by her whirling thoughts.

That morning she had awakened a spinster; a spinster, moreover, with no chance in the world of contracting a suitable match. Less than eight hours later she was on the arm of a handsome young man who professed a desire to marry her despite her drawbacks of indifferent looks and utter poverty. And all this confusion had come about because Annabella Winter had been rude to her cousin in the street.

Mary decided on the spot that the world was so odd a place that there was no point in trying to understand it.

Lady Winter instantly secured the best private parlour the Red Lion could boast; Mary gathered that her aunt was known in this historic public house, being in the habit of repairing here with some of her gentleman sporting friends after a horse auction. Uncle Egbert would have an apoplexy if he knew, but for the moment Aunt's notoriety in the house was welcome.

Lady Winter's party was ushered into the cosy, chintz-trimmed parlour without even a second of the waiting which usually attended such ceremonies. Mary was glad to get herself and her ruin of a dress so quickly away from prying eyes. She was having enough difficulty in dealing with the warm, speculative glance of Ramirez.

Lady Winter indicated that the young people should join her around an oaken table in the centre of the room. This they did, Ramirez holding a chair for each lady in turn with what Mary considered an over-smoothness. When they were seated, Mary spoke.

"Aunt—" she looked earnestly into the steel-grey eyes of the elder lady "—how can you even contemplate this? I can't simply marry the first man I meet in the street."

"That, by your account, would have been the unconscious chap. Looked rather coarse to me," returned Aunt Winter.

Mary often enjoyed her aunt's wit, but this was not one of those occasions. "All your trouble is for nothing, Aunt," she said crossly. "I'm much past the age when I need to please anyone but myself in such a personal matter. And I don't intend to go through any ceremony with this gentleman, today or any other day."

Mary's plain speaking took Lady Winter momentarily aback, despite all her arrangements. Ramirez was also silent, and Mary didn't dare to look at him.

His was the next voice to sound in the room. "My very dear Miss Winter," he said in a slow, deliberate way that made Mary turn to him, almost against her will, "are you so anxious to spend your life a single lady? Your esteemed aunt must know more of your English customs than either of us, and she thinks that you can never marry after today's spectacle. Yet here I am, not only willing, but eager to make you my wife. Wouldn't that be better than a lifetime of—what do they say?—ah, yes, single blessedness?"

"Good points, the pair of you," put in Aunt Winter. "You'll have lovely children."

Mary turned red as a rose and cast down her eyes. When she looked up, it was directly at Ramirez. "Why, sir, did you conceive this sudden desire to marry me? Or to marry anyone? It would seem to me that your circumstances don't permit it, unless there's a lot more money in fencing instruction than I think. And you know that I can contribute nothing."

"It is my duty, as your countryman, to protect your good name," was the instant answer. Ramirez flashed a burning look at her. "And there would be many advantages for me."

Mary willed herself not to blush again. "Not the least of which, probably, is living off my relations," she retorted to disguise her confusion. "Well, my Papa and I are doing that already. The Winter family would not welcome another mouth to feed, no matter how skilled in flattery that mouth is."

"Mary!" admonished Lady Winter. "Naturally your husband will be welcome in our home, and Sir Egbert shall find him a nice genteel post so he may quit that meagre fencing business."

"As for you, Madam—" Mary turned to her aunt "—I know very well that you think this a welcome turn of events. You won't have to present me to society now. Well, I never expected you to. Please, Aunt, let's go off to meet Annabella and forget this nonsense. As for the scandal, it will only be a nine days' wonder."

"I wouldn't be too sure. No young lady, to my knowledge, has ever had her clothes ripped off in Tattersall's."

"I did not have my clothes—"

Ramirez's low chuckle drowned out Mary's outrage. "Lady Winter, if I may be so bold," he said, flashing a smile at the elder lady, "I think I can bring your niece round. It needs only a short private interview with her. You permit?"

"Well!" sniffed Lady Winter. Mary, whose nerves jumped at the idea of a private talk with Ramirez, breathed a sigh of relief as she saw her aunt's dignity reassert itself. "You're asking me to wait in the corridor, I suppose. Young man, you forget yourself."

"I ask nothing of the kind of so gracious a lady. Miss Winter and I will go into the corridor. What I have to say will but take a moment."

"Hmmph." Lady Winter glared at Ramirez for one penetrating instant. Then, "Mary, child, go with him," she directed with an odd glint in her eye.

"No," said Mary.

"Come, my dearest young lady, you cannot deny me one word with you. And in the corridor, with maidservants bumping into us, you can't fear for your safety."

"Oh, go on, Mary, he can't bite you," said Lady Winter.

"And I must remember, I'm already ruined," Mary added sweetly, but she got up from her chair and preceded Ramirez out of the parlour.

Once the door was safely closed behind them, Mary faced Ramirez with her most pleading expression and addressed him in Spanish. She was glad they had taken this way to privacy, for the corridor was by no means empty and she had nothing to fear from being alone with him. Waitresses laden with trays of drink pelted past, and the occasional gentleman eased by the couple. "*Señor,* please stop plaguing me. Go about your business and forget these notions of honour, or whatever is making you behave so dreadfully." She hesitated. "It would be easiest for all of us if you didn't return to my aunt. Please. Simply leave us now."

"But, my dear, I know what is distressing you. You believe I want to marry you to force my, er, attentions on you. I brought you out here to swear to you that no such thing is in my mind. I won't pursue my husbandly rights without your leave; you have my word on that. And as long as it is unconsummated, I believe the marriage could be set aside if you should decide that is best."

"Oh." Mary was surprised at the little sinking feeling in the pit of her stomach. She had surmised that if he didn't want money—and she didn't see how he could believe a marriage with her would be lucrative, unless he counted living off the Winter family as great riches—perhaps he wanted her for her charms? It had been a silly hope, and he had effectively dashed it. By marrying her he would simply be acting out of gallantry.

Or would he? Ramirez's dark eyes were smiling down into Mary's. "I swear to you, my dear, I will never come to your bed unless you invite me there yourself," he whispered. His tone was sensuous, caressing.

"And I would never invite you to come within ten yards of me," Mary retorted at her most snappish. His air of intimacy brought out her instinct for self-protection. He was practically a stranger. How could he have such power over her, forcing her to think such unseemly thoughts of bedchambers and conjugal mysteries? "I can't marry you. And that, sir, is final."

Ramirez smiled. He looked into her eyes, and Mary felt, uneasily, that he could see right through her protests to her undeniable attraction to him. "A man can but try. Let's return you to your aunt." And before Mary could say anything else, he had opened the door to the private parlour.

"Well?" Aunt Winter's eyes were bright with query.

Mary shrugged.

Ramirez said, "I have removed the last doubt in your niece's mind, Madam. She will marry me. We think it best that the ceremony be this very day."

"What? I never—"

Lady Winter and Ramirez discussed wedding plans, ignoring Mary's protests.

"You, sir, are not an honourable man," Mary finally had to shout into the middle of the pair's discussion of the nearest Catholic church. They would be married by a priest, of course. Ramirez did insist upon that.

Ramirez caught at her hand and captured it. "On the contrary, my dear, I am acting in our best interests. I understand that you are a logical and practical young lady. Naturally you must refuse an offer from a stranger. You have told me you can't marry me. But can you look me in the eye and say that you don't want to be my wife?"

Mary was stunned. Could he—did he want to marry her so much that he would insist in this way? It was a heady feeling. No man had ever asked for her hand. Reminding herself that no man but this one ever would, thanks to the unfortunate events of the day, she hesitated.

What would she lose by this wedding? She had to admit that the bridegroom who stood before her had been filling her dreams of late. She had always been a secret romantic. If left to herself without the conventions of the world to cling to—those conservative notions which would scoff at a marriage based on a few hours' acquaintance—she suspected that she would marry him in an instant. And chance was offering her the opportunity to do precisely that.

She looked him in the eye, as he had asked, and nearly gasped at the expression she found there. "Do you truly promise not to..." She tried to go on but found herself quite unable to voice her one fear in front of Lady Winter.

He understood her. He bowed, kissing her hand in its glove. His lips seemed to burn through the service-able York tan. "Never, except at your invitation."

Mary shivered; not only his eyes, but his voice, seemed full of a certainty that he would not have long to wait before she invited him into her bedchamber.

"Here, now, children, enough time for that sort of thing after the knot's tied," said Lady Winter. She beamed on her niece. "Disposed of in one day! Never fear, my love, I'll buy you a new dress, anyway. And won't we show that snip Annabella a thing or two?"

For the first time, Mary believed that she would really end the day as the wife of Antonio Ramirez y Mondego. The picture was not altogether unpleasant, especially with her cousin's discontented face in the foreground.

Still, she was confirmed in her opinion that there was no comprehending this strange world. It seemed absurd that she had once thought England would be a safe place compared to the Peninsula.

CHAPTER SIX

THE REST OF THE MORNING was a blur to Mary. First Lords Cathcott and Stephens arrived, Cathcott waving the special license, Stephens bearing assurances from Lord Holland that young Ramirez y Mondego was the best of fellows, a diplomatist of the rarest order, besides being of a noble Spanish family—though, unfortunately, fallen upon hard times.

"We knew that," snapped Lady Winter. "Works for a living, don't he? Blood will tell, though."

Mary focussed her attention on the world around her long enough to wonder what her aunt meant by that particular cliché.

Next came the hackney ride to St. Patrick's church in Soho Square and the hunting up of a harrassed-looking priest. Mary was momentarily relieved when this cleric informed them that, special license or no, the couple was too late to be wed in the church that day, and that, furthermore, all English marriages had to be solemnized by a minister of the Church of England.

This disappointment didn't make Ramirez hesitate to go through with the ceremony. "Later, when we go home to Spain, my dear, a priest shall say words over

us," he said. "We will do what must be done, mean-
time, to satisfy the strange demands of this country."

"Queer start, if you ask me," grumbled Lady Winter. "Back to the Red Lion then, children, and we'll
find ourselves a vicar."

Thus it was that Mary eventually found herself
standing before a rumpled city clergyman in the private parlour of an inn, not even a church.

"Poor girl, this is not the stuff dreams are made
of," Ramirez whispered to her as they took their
places.

Mary grimaced. Perhaps he had seen her face fall.
A hurried wedding in a strange place, the bride in a
torn gown, the groom in morning dress and carrying
a foil! This was so far from being her dream that it was
almost ludicrous.

Even with the unfamiliar English words, Mary recognized the marriage service as she might an old
friend. As a very young girl she had been known to
recite it over to herself, wondering if she would ever
make those sacred vows aloud, and to whom. She was
dimly aware of the clarity and seeming sincerity of
Ramirez's thrilling voice as he made his responses; she
tried to rise to the occasion and at least managed to
keep her own voice from quaking.

Then it was done! Mary, quite suddenly, was a
countess of the Spanish realm.

Lady Winter marched ahead of the bridal pair out
into Crown Passage. "Done at last, children! You're
as married as can be." She turned to her niece, her face
breaking out in a smile. "Won't Annabella stare when

she hears me call you Lady—what was your name
again, young man? Oh, yes—Lady Ramirez.''

"It isn't the custom in Spain for a married lady to
give up her name," said Mary, lifting her chin. "There
I would be called the Countess *de* Ramirez, but remain Mary Winter."

"Hah! Strange thing, that. Well, you're in England, Niece, and that makes you Lady Ramirez in my
book."

"It hardly matters, considering the odd kind of
marriage this is," replied Mary with a shrug. She
thought she intercepted a hurt look in Ramirez's eyes
and turned her face away resolutely. Her emotions
were racing this way and that. How could she have
done it, actually tied herself to a stranger?

The newly united pair stepped, after Lady Winter,
into a hackney coach in Pall Mall. Paul the footman
jumped up onto the box, and Lady Winter shouted out
the window with her usual vigour, "Layton and
Shears', and make these daisy-cutters step lively,
man!"

It was only then that Mary remembered Annabella
was still in town, doubtless wondering what had become of her mother, if not of her cousin Mary.

"Ah, you're in for a treat, Ramirez," said Lady
Winter as the Spaniard assisted her out of the coach in
front of the draper's. "Ever see a young woman of
quality have a fit of the vapours in public? My
daughter should give us a rare show."

"Aunt," said Mary with a shudder. The thought of
such a spectacle gave her no pleasure, however gleeful
the prospect made Lady Winter. Mary had had em-

barrassing scenes enough to last her a lifetime. "Perhaps we shouldn't tell Annabella."

"Not tell her? What's she to think when we bring this young man home in the carriage with us, then, and give him a room in the house?"

"Heavens, is that what you intend to do?" gasped Mary. She had somehow imagined that, the marriage safely done, Ramirez would return to his lodging and go about his business, as would she. They might meet once, months or even years from now, to discuss an annulment.

"We can hardly leave him on the street corner. Family's family, ain't that so, my boy?" Lady Winter gave Ramirez a poke.

He flashed a grin. "My Lady, you are a wonder," he exclaimed. "And I will delight in meeting your charming daughter. If she takes after you, I'm certain I shall be overwhelmed."

"If she took after me I'd have drunk poison years ago," muttered Lady Winter, following this statement with a harsh cackle. "Now take your wife's arm. Come, Mary. Here's a sight for Annabella!"

Lady Winter strode into the shop, looking eagerly about her for her daughter or James, the very tall second footman. Behind her came Mary and Ramirez. While Lady Winter scoured every corner of the establishment, Mary and her new husband stood uncertainly in the middle of the place, Mary observing with an interested eye the bustle of activity all about her as shop assistants reached down bolts of cloth from high shelves for this or that fashionable female customer. Layton and Shears' was the absolute opposite of Tattersall's. Had it not been for the assistants, the occasional lady's footman, and Ramirez, the draper's would have been an exclusively feminine precinct.

"Why, Mary." The voice was familiar, though its cooing tone was less so. Annabella, all smiles and fluttering eyelashes, was hurrying to her cousin's side. "Do introduce me to your charming friend. Oh!" that young lady gasped, as her shrewd, light blue eyes took in the wreckage of Mary's costume. "What have you done to your gown?"

"Nothing. You must remember, the torn front breadth is the latest fashion in the Peninsula. How odd, Annabella, for you to be demanding introductions from me when you're so reluctant to return the favour."

Annabella laughed, a brittle, tinkling sound. "Sir," she said, addressing Ramirez and maintaining her brilliant smile, "you must excuse my dear cousin. We had the tiniest misunderstanding earlier, and she hasn't forgotten it yet. I have, of course. I'm never one to hold a grudge."

Mary seethed, rolling her eyes heavenward. She glanced at Ramirez, wondering if she would see the besotted expression so many men exhibited when confronted by Annabella's overripe charms. To her surprise and secret relief, Ramirez's handsome face registered amusement and nothing more.

"You must be the cousin I've heard so much about." He addressed Annabella, bestowing upon her a smile which Mary could tell was more devastating to the female sex than any weapon Annabella had in her pitched battle with the peace of the world's males.

Annabella brought up the full artillery neverthe-less, lowering her eyelids for a demure moment, then looking up with an even sweeter smile. "Oh! You've heard of me."

"Your charming mother is most eloquent in your...praise," returned Ramirez.

At this Annabella made a little moue of dissatisfac-tion, but she recovered quickly. "You've met Mama?" Out of the side of her mouth, she whispered to Mary, "Introduce me!"

Mary knew that further delay would be useless, but she was determined to disconcert Annabella all she could. "This is Count Ramirez y Mondego. *Señor conde,* my cousin Miss Winter. Lord Ramirez is a fencing master, Annabella."

Choking back a giggle, Mary then watched emo-tions war on Annabella's transparent features. A count—respect! A fencing master—disdain! One could see Annabella try to reconcile the two and de-cide on a proper demeanour.

The title of count finally decided the matter as An-nabella purred, "A fencing master! How interesting, sir. I've heard that many aristocrats have their little eccentricities. There is that Lord What's-his-name who drives a coach, you know. And—"

Ramirez cut her off. "I make my living by it, Madam. Ah!" He looked over the young ladies' heads. "Here comes your charming mother."

It was the second time he had called Lady Winter charming; Mary was surprised to find that the adjec-tive, usually not applied to her no-nonsense aunt, sounded less odd with repetition.

Before the girls could so much as turn round, Lady Winter was upon them. "Drat!" was her greeting. "Missed it. Well, Annabella, what do you think of your new cousin?"

"New cousin?" Annabella's face betrayed complete bewilderment.

"I didn't tell her," Mary murmured softly in the direction of her aunt's bonnet.

"Capital! Saved it for me to do," cried Lady Winter with a wink. "Annabella, your cousin was married today. She is now the Countess de Ramirez."

Annabella's normally round eyes widened even more; she let out a shriek and gazed from Mary to the handsome Spanish count with the same expression she might have used had she been confronted with a man-eating lion. Several shoppers turned to stare. For the first time, Mary was completely satisfied with her marriage.

"But—but—" Annabella spluttered, searching for words. "He is only a fencing master!" she finally cried in triumph. "They will starve."

"Not likely, my dear. They're coming home with us now to Woodbank Hall, and your father will find dear Antonio a place worthy of his talents. Sir Egbert does have a connection or two. Something in government, perhaps, if they let foreigners in."

"Coming home! To live with us? Why..." Annabella's mouth dropped open, fishlike. Then she turned to Mary. "How odd, Cousin, that you never mentioned your betrothed. I had no idea this was your wedding day!"

"Nor did I," said Mary.

Explanations were in order, and Lady Winter, for one, knew that hiding the sordid details of the match from Annabella would be useless. All society would be buzzing with the affair by nightfall, and as if that weren't enough, Paul the footman had seen the whole thing. Lady Winter was aware that her daughter gossiped with the servants, and, with an air of resignation, she explained matters simply and truthfully. In an effort to sweeten the tale in Mary's favour, she did elaborate a little on Ramirez's violent desire to wed her niece.

Mary and Ramirez stood silently by during the story, Mary admiring the lady's sense of drama.

"Oh, a scandal!" Annabella found her voice when her mother had come to the end. "That's different."

"Indeed it is," agreed Lady Winter. "The children will have to be careful as can be to show themselves in public and whatnot, so that tongues won't wag further. Hope they don't take the shine out of your appearance, daughter. Well, it's a shocking squeeze in here. Have you made your purchases? I saw James weighted down like the Brighton stage. Let's be off home and break the news to Captain Winter and your father. Come, my dears."

She sailed away through the crowd of milling shoppers. Ramirez gave Mary his arm, offered the other to Annabella as if in afterthought—which Mary could not but appreciate—and the little group followed in awkward silence.

MARY TIPTOED into her father's bedroom later on that same day. She had run to see him as soon as the coach stopped at the front sweep, leaving her aunt and cousin to welcome Ramirez to the house. Mary meant to break the news of her marriage to Papa in a gentle way suitable to his indifferent state of health, and she must do it at once, before he heard the news from someone else.

Captain Winter looked up from his nest in the bed. Spread upon the coverlet was a forest of newspapers, and a large map of the Peninsula lay in his lap. He had been marking on it with a pencil, Mary knew, keeping up with Wellington's movements in the only way he could. "Well, what is it, Daughter? What the devil did you do to your gown?"

Mary remembered that she hadn't stopped to change into a less shocking costume; she clutched the torn breadth as she had been doing throughout the day. "Well, Papa, it's rather complicated. I was married today."

"What?" roared Captain Winter, scattering papers. He kept staring at his daughter's gown. "I'll kill the wretch!"

"Oh, it's nothing like that," said Mary quickly, aghast at where his thoughts had led. She hadn't exactly broken the news gently. Her father's face was already turning an apoplectic red. She had to continue, though; she had already said too much.

In as simple a manner as she knew how, she related the day's incidents. "You see, Papa, nobody else in the world will marry me now," she finished. "We're to put it about that this gentleman and I have been betrothed, in hopes of scotching the scandal somewhat. And he assured me that he would not—that our marriage will be platonic so that we can set it aside later if I should prefer."

"Caught in the middle of a brawl in Tattersall's," Captain Winter said in awe. He had grown calmer as Mary told her story, but his expression still registered incredulity. "Bring a girl up right with a duenna, and what does it serve? I told you it was no use guarding her like the crown jewels, Inez." He seemed to exchange a look with Mama's portrait above the mantelpiece, then turned to Mary with a stern frown. "Well? What's the name of this young man you say was so chivalrous as to take you with no dowry, no good name, no nothing? Sounds havey-cavey to me. Fencing master! He's bound to be some counterjumper out to better his lot. Married! If I'd had any idea you would come home married today...don't you know he'll have all your fortune now by law?"

"But I have nothing," said Mary. Indeed, her penniless circumstances had figured largely in her decision to go through with the marriage. She knew for a fact that her husband couldn't be a fortune hunter.

"Well, it's the principle of the thing," said Captain Winter. "Tell me the fellow's name, and be quick about it."

"He is a Spanish gentleman," said Mary. "You would have met him at Lord Holland's, Papa, if you hadn't been taken ill. I told you about him. You remember, the young man who helped us out to the carriage. He turns out to be an impoverished count, and his name is Antonio Ramirez y Mondego."

"What?" Captain Winter stared and fell back among the bedclothes. "A Spanish fellow, and of that family. It lacked only that." He muttered the last words, then closed his eyes as if in pain.

"Papa?" Mary rushed to the bed, afraid that her father had fainted. When she was near enough she could see that his eyes were squeezed shut.

He opened them to glare up at her. "Do you know, young woman, what a fool you've been?"

Since she knew that, on many levels, she had indeed been foolish, Mary was hard put to give him an answer.

Before she could even begin to try, a knock sounded on the door. Mary called out, "Enter," without thinking.

Ramirez walked into the room. "I hope I am not intruding, but I felt time might be of the essence here. What you have to relate to your father is so upsetting that I might be of some support...."

"You!" Captain Winter sat upright and regarded Ramirez with a murderous stare. "You think you've been clever, don't you? A Ramirez, of all the blasted luck. Well, think again. My daughter and I are going into town this instant to get this marriage annulled. Mary, change into another dress. Can't have you flitting about the town looking as if you've been ravished." The captain hopped out of bed, revealing spindly legs under a well-worn nightshirt, and staggered as he hit the carpet.

Mary and Ramirez both jumped to help him. "Papa, you know you can't be out of bed. You're not yet well," said Mary. "What is amiss? Do you know each other?" She addressed the last words as much to Ramirez as to her father.

Ramirez appeared to be honestly unknowing as he shook his head.

"I know *of* him," puffed Captain Winter, struggling in the young people's hands. "He won't grow richer over this marriage, my girl, you may be sure of that." Then the captain's shoulders sagged as apparent dizziness overcame him. Only the tight grip Ramirez had on him saved him from falling to the floor.

"Once again you've come to my father's aid," said Mary to Ramirez a little later. She had rung for a maid, and together she and Ramirez had put Captain Winter back to bed. Papa was muttering incoherently, and Mary didn't know if this relapse was genuine or no; his fever hadn't returned. Now she looked at Ramirez keenly. "I apologize for my father's behaviour. He must be quite upset to think that you might get practical good out of this marriage. Had I a fortune, I might understand his reaction, but as I don't..."

"I have no idea," said Ramirez. "He served in Spain; perhaps he distrusts people of my country."

"That can hardly be the case, sir. He married my mother."

"Ah, yes. Inez de la Rosa." Ramirez's eyes found the portrait over the mantel. "The loveliest creature in all Spain in her time. You look like her."

"I do not, sir, and I refuse to fall victim to your cajoling ways," said Mary, eyes flashing. He had hit upon a sore point; she had always wished to resemble her beautiful mother, and, though her father maintained that she had a look of Inez about her, she couldn't see it. "When Papa comes to himself, I'll be certain to ask him why he distrusts you. He seemed to think it worse that you were a Ramirez than anything else.''

"What can I say, my dear? My family is of the utmost respectability and has been for centuries. You may ask anyone you wish, and so may your father.''

Mary nodded, but her uncertainty must have shown in her face.

Ramirez caught the look. "Then you will be obtaining that annulment? I fear it won't be as simple as the captain thinks. One doesn't go into town and buy such a thing at a counter.''

"I . . .'' Mary didn't know what to say to this. If her father ordered her to annul the marriage and it was in her power to do so, how could she refuse? On the other hand . . .

"You are of age," said Ramirez. He was speaking softly, his glance straying from time to time to the inert form of Captain Winter. "You might remain my wife if it is your wish.''

Mary also observed her father. Did his eyelids flicker at this suggestion? Confusion overcame her. She looked into Ramirez's eyes, wishing it were as easy to see into his heart.

"Well, my dear?" he said softly, with a little smile.

The maid's entrance saved Mary from having to answer. She had to forget her own problems to concentrate on her father's. She was relieved that no direct question could be asked of her now. Ramirez bowed himself out of the room without another word, and with only one enigmatic glance.

Mary was left to fret over Papa's stubborn refusal to return to consciousness. He didn't look very ill to her, and she more than half suspected that he was feigning insensibility, probably to avoid his daughter.

"Oh, Papa," said Mary with a sigh when the maid had left them alone. "Why did you make such a fuss?"

But Captain Winter stayed silent on this most important subject.

CHAPTER SEVEN

WHEN MARY WALKED into the drawing room later that evening, after an unsuccessful vigil at Papa's bedside and a quick change of clothes, she wasn't surprised to find all eyes fixed upon her. What did shock her was that the room was full of people. She hadn't remembered that the Winters were giving a dinner party.

Silence reigned as Mary paused by the door. Then an excited buzz of conversation swept the room. Mary took a deep breath and started for the place where her aunt was sitting, a settle by the massive stone fireplace. She managed friendly smiles for the guests she passed. At first glance she could see the vicar and his lady; Squire Evans, his plump wife and giggling, reed-thin daughters; and fusty Lord Burnham, the master of the local hunt and of Hilltop House, the great house of the neighbourhood.

Someone stepped in front of Mary. "Miss Winter. Er, I mean, Lady Ramirez. Lady Winter was telling us you were married today. Sudden, wasn't it? We none of us knew you was betrothed."

Mary looked up, startled, into the broad red face of John St. Charles, Annabella's latest conquest. Mary had met the young man, Lord Burnham's house-guest, but once before, when he had paid a call on

Annabella. She was astonished that he should single
her out. So, apparently, was Annabella, who, though
caught in a chattering knot of Evans girls, was able to
spare Mary a glare from across the room.

"My marriage was indeed unexpected, sir," said
Mary, eyeing St. Charles with some suspicion. She
thought him perfect for her cousin, which didn't say
much for her opinion of him. So tall and broad that he
made even Annabella look tiny by comparison, St.
Charles, with his straw-coloured hair and ruddy
cheeks, was the epitome of the bluff young sportsman.

Mary knew Lady Winter was fond of him already
and hoped for everyone's sake that he would ask for
Annabella's hand. He would spoil everything if he
appeared to flirt with Mary; and Annabella would
surely see any kind of attention, no matter how slight,
as flirtation.

The thought ran through Mary's mind that her new
status as a married woman might make her a safe tar-
get for empty gallantries; she had never experienced
any before. How, she wondered, could she get away
from this young man without being rude?

St. Charles, smiling broadly, said, "I'd wager
you've disappointed many a young man in the neighbourhood, Madam."

Mary's jaw nearly dropped as she groped for some
answer to this. She would be shocked if any young
man in the county so much as knew she was alive. If
this was gallantry, she didn't like it; compliments
should have at least the appearance of truth.

"My dear fellow, this is a disappointment you must learn to live with," said a familiar voice. Mary spun round to find Ramirez, handsomer than ever in neat evening attire, standing by with a suave smile on his face.

"I didn't know you were here," said Mary.

"I just came in; Lady Winter was good enough to send for my things from town, and I had to wait to dress," said Ramirez. He put a proprietary arm around Mary's waist, nodding at St. Charles. "But never mind; I won't be the kind of husband who objects to his wife engaging in a harmless bit of flirtation."

"Flirtation!" Mary wriggled a little in an effort to disengage his arm, but he held her tight. "This gentleman and I are barely acquainted, sir."

St. Charles grinned. "Still, as I was telling the lady, sir, you've stolen a march on many merely by being on the spot."

"Our marriage might have been a little rushed by the events of the day, but that is all," said Ramirez. "We've been acquainted for ages, you know."

"So I am led to believe," St. Charles began, when he was hailed by Lady Winter and Lord Burnham, who had been engaging in a rough conversation concerning the breeding of hounds and now loudly demanded his opinion.

"Well, my dear," said Ramirez into Mary's ear, speaking in Spanish, "you never told me you had an admirer."

"I don't," answered Mary at once. "He's one of Annabella's flirts."

"And who is he? You didn't introduce us."

"Mr. St. Charles, a guest of Lord Burnham's."

"Ah! So that is the famous Mr. St. Charles." Ramirez looked after the burly young man with an odd light in his eyes.

"Famous? Could you have heard of him? He's quite an ordinary young man, or so I would suppose. Rides to hounds and likes Annabella, quite in the style of most young men in the neighbourhood."

"Your cousin mentioned him as one of her devoted admirers," said Ramirez. "Weren't you listening to her conversation in the chaise?"

"I try not to, for I've heard it all before," returned Mary with a smile. She glanced round at the company, noticing that the bright stares of many of the guests were still fixed upon her. "I suppose I must take you round and present you to these people; according to Mr. St. Charles, Lady Winter has regaled the room with our story already, and we can be sure she hasn't put it delicately."

"Good of her to spare us the trouble, don't you agree?" said Ramirez, lifting Mary's hand to kiss it. "Lead me to the slaughter. You have a wonderful collection of neighbours, by the way. Quite in the English style. And all of them looking most anxious to speak to us."

Mary shot him an irritated look. She suspected he was amused by this outrageous predicament. "I must tell you honestly, sir, that my father's distress about our marriage has made me a bit uneasy. Are you certain you can't explain why he should object so strongly?"

Ramirez shrugged. "I cannot. But what father would want to lose his daughter so suddenly? I wouldn't wish a daughter of mine to marry a stranger. I have every hope that when Captain Winter fully understands the situation he will welcome me as his son. And now, my dear, don't you think we should get on with this chore? Your cousin rather resembles a cabbage rose surrounded by blades of tall grass; those young ladies she is with are extremely slender. Their mother should not dress them all in green. Shall we let them be the first to hear the story of our day at Tattersall's?"

"You may be sure they've already heard all about it," returned Mary, repressing the urge to laugh at his wicked description of Annabella and the Evans girls. "What they really want to know is why any gentleman in his right mind would marry me."

"Let us show them," said Ramirez, and to Mary's shock he bent to kiss her cheek very tenderly, which bold action brought on a renewed burst of chatter from the guests.

THE REST OF THE EVENING was as uncomfortable for Mary as a clutch of curious neighbours could make it. The owlish and silent young curate was her dinner partner, which made it impossible for her to forward her acquaintance with her new husband. Ramirez was placed directly across from Mary at table. Though he had taken in Lady Stanhope, a deaf and crusty dowager, Annabella, on his other side, monopolized him and ignored her own dinner partner, Squire Evans.

"I suppose you have a castle in Spain, sir," said Annabella with an affected giggle and a practiced plying of eyelashes.

"Yes, *señorita,* I do, but I sometimes wonder if I shall see it again." Ramirez kept his eyes on his plate, Mary noticed, and she respected him for resisting Annabella's wiles.

"Heavens! Why not simply go and see it?"

"Because, my dear young lady, my country is under siege." Ramirez nearly snapped out these words, but Annabella didn't seem to notice his intensity. She merely gave him a nod as a signal that he should continue his story.

Mary was listening intently by now.

"One day I may see my home again, if Bonaparte's brother is chased off the throne of Spain. You cannot feature, Miss Winter, what a blow it was to the Spanish mind when that upstart replaced our king."

"Boney's brother. Fancy the monster having brothers," said Annabella in a fashionably drawling voice. Her lack of interest in the Spanish problem was evident. In truth, she had heard it all before, as had Mary, for Sir Egbert and Captain Winter made it their practice to argue over the Spanish question. Captain Winter maintained that the Spanish quest for a constitutional monarchy would come to nothing. Sir Egbert expressed his doubts on that score also, but insisted that the Spanish must have their chance to be ruled by the king they wanted. Ramirez went on with his talk, tending to follow Sir Egbert's reasoning, though in an infinitely more dramatic way.

Annabella soon elected to turn this dry-as-dust subject. "Why, Count Ramirez! I would never have put you down for such a prosy fellow. Surely there are more *attractive* things much closer to you to discuss."

Mary was guilty of lifting her eyebrows. So was Ramirez. Their eyes met.

Ramirez continued to address Annabella, but he kept his eyes on Mary. "Someday soon, Miss Winter, we will succeed in returning our king Fernando to the throne. One of the corrupt Bourbons, alas, but the only king we have. He will accept the Constitution of Cadiz, and better times will come to Spain. We will succeed, Miss Winter."

Annabella's interest was not piqued. "As you say, but tell me, sir, what do you think of my gown?" she asked in her most flirtatious manner.

Ramirez smiled slightly at Mary before turning to assure his new cousin that he found her gown of blush-pink sarcenet most striking.

When the guests left at last, and the family was alone in the drawing room, Mary finally had leisure to consider what her uncle must think of the day's happenings. She was afraid that she had lost all hope of winning his good opinion. She hadn't even dared to meet his eyes at dinner. Not that that would have done any good, the gathering having turned Sir Egbert into his usual social self, a completely silent man who studied his plate at all times.

Lady Winter brought up the topic uppermost in the family's thoughts. "Now, Sir Egbert, what do you think of this start of Mary's? Handled it well, didn't

I? A countess in one day, upon my word. It ain't every matchmaker who's so successful.''

"It's a bit irregular, to be sure," said Sir Egbert. Those blue eyes, so like Captain Winter's, turned to Mary at last. "It does get you established in a way, Niece. Young Ramirez here is a decent sort. And if you don't dislike him, many marriages of convenience turn out very happily."

"Ours was an arranged match; never set eyes on Sir Egbert till the day he came to ask for my hand," Lady Winter put in.

"And what an example it will be to us," was Ramirez's contribution.

Mary jumped at the sound of her husband's voice. He was smiling at her, the picture of innocence. There was something in his eyes... could it be an imitation of husbandly devotion? She wondered how Sir Egbert could know whether Ramirez was "decent" or not.

"I'm so confused," said Mary to her uncle.

"My dear, naturally you are," returned Sir Egbert. "Not least of your confusions is my brother's reaction to your nuptials. Heard about it from my valet; how the servants know all they do is beyond me. Mark my words, Niece, your father will come round."

Mary had never heard such a long speech from her uncle; she stared at him in surprise. All the world besides Papa seemed united to defend Antonio Ramirez.

"Naturally George will come round," said Lady Winter, confirming Mary's impression. "He ain't a fool. Here's his daughter a countess, and with no trouble to himself. Give him a day or two to settle down, Mary, and he'll think this marriage a blessing. Oh." Lady Winter put her hand to her head. "Stap me if I hadn't forgotten all about it. Your things, Mary, have been moved to the Queen's Chambers."

"Why, thank you, Aunt," said Mary in surprise.

"What?" protested Annabella. "Mary has a perfectly good room, Mama."

"Not for a married lady. No squawking from you, daughter. Had you come home with a husband I would have moved your things in there. It's tradition for brides of the family."

Annabella's eyes snapped in anger. The Queen's Chambers, so named because Good Queen Bess had once made a change of costume at Woodbank Hall on her route to somewhere else, were the closest the Hall boasted to rooms of state. And Mary was to sleep there!

Sir Egbert, who was sitting next to his wife, coughed and murmured something in her ear.

"Oh. Yes, of course." Lady Winter frowned, then beckoned Mary with one crooked finger. "You, girl. I'll take you upstairs first. Your young man can join you a little later. Annabella! See that you entertain the boy properly."

"Oh, to be sure, Mama," chirped Annabella. Suddenly in a much better mood, she cast a flirtatious look at Ramirez.

Mary endured the too-hearty good-night of her uncle, Annabella's toss of the head, and Ramirez's teasing glance before she followed her aunt out of the room. She feared she could guess why the lady was accompanying her.

At the massive door to the Queen's Bedchamber, Lady Winter motioned Mary inside. "I'll join you in a moment, my dear. Have to go to my own room and, er, get something."

"Very well, Aunt." Mary was relieved. Perhaps the elder lady had decided to forego the dreaded lecture on the Marriage Bed in favour of a hasty retreat and a message sent by her maid.

Aunt Winter hurried down the corridor, and Mary turned the handle to the bedchamber. Once inside, she had to pause and look about her in amusement and delight. She had visited these chambers before, but she hadn't imagined that she would ever stay in them. She walked from room to room: there were four, each opening into the next. She went first to the large bedroom, hung with faded tapestries of hunting scenes and boasting a high, historic bed with a scarlet brocade covering. A stiff portrait of Good Queen Bess seemed to leer down from over a mantelpiece carved with cupids, gargoyles, and other creatures of fancy, and the parquet floor was covered by a Persian carpet of such antiquity that it could well have dated from the seventeenth century.

Opening off the bedchamber was a sort of sitting room, though it had more the look of an audience chamber with its thronelike, gilded chair on a dais and the smaller chairs ranged round the edges of the room. The walls of the sitting room housed a terrifying collection of animal heads and bits of antique weaponry left over from the front hall of the house. There was a small inner chamber that might serve as a gentleman's dressing room if the need arose. When Mary peeked in, she saw a collection of trunks and boxes. Here, then, was where Ramirez would be sleeping.

Finally she returned to the antechamber. The family's decorative ingenuity seemed to have come to a halt in this small, bare room ornamented with a couple of trestle tables and a wooden bench or two. The gloom was offset by some fine leaded-glass windows, one of which had a stained-glass centre representing Queen Elizabeth with one dainty foot atop a miniature ship of the Spanish Armada.

It was in the antechamber that Aunt Winter found Mary. "There you are, my dear. Now come back to the bedroom and we'll talk."

Mary choked back the urge to laugh and hurried after her aunt. The older woman was clutching a white garment in one hand, and the military cast of her walk made it clear that her ladyship was nervous about the moments to come.

The two women settled into X-shaped chairs facing the cheerful bedroom fire. Aunt Winter cleared her throat. "Well, Mary, you've had no mother for a number of years now..." she began. Her harsh features crimsoned over.

Mary could stand it no longer. She had never seen her aunt change colour. "Oh, dear Aunt, this isn't necessary. Before she died my Mama told me all about—about men and women."

Aunt Winter brightened. "Did she now? The marriage bed and all that?"

"Indeed, yes," said Mary, a little smile flitting across her face as she remembered that long-ago conversation. She had been shocked and certain her mother must be making an error about the mechanics of the matter; either that or the spiritual side of married love, upon which Doña Inez had insisted, meant that the physical must be less awkward than the explanation seemed to indicate.

"Well!" Aunt Winter's wide smile almost made Mary laugh. "Your uncle thought someone should warn you, but glad I am your mama was man enough—er, good enough—to get to you before I could. Now I've only one thing to give you, and I'll be going." She held up the white garment she had been carrying, and Mary saw that it was a severe linen nightdress, buttoned high at the neck and yellowed with age. "From my wedding night to Sir Egbert. I'll help you change into it for luck."

"Why, thank you, Aunt." Mary held back another laugh. As Aunt Winter helped Mary unhook her dress and change into the linen sack, which was long enough to put its young wearer in danger of tripping over her feet, Mary reflected that the gown would certainly be appropriate for her mission this night: to remain a chaste maiden. She wondered how it had done for that genuine wedding night long ago.

"Good night, Niece, and mind you behave yourself," was Aunt Winter's parting advice. She turned the shade of a beet as she uttered it and escaped from the room.

Mary finally gave vent to a fit of the giggles. Then she crossed to the nearest pier glass and took a good look at herself. She doubted that Ramirez would really enter this room, since he had promised not to claim his husbandly rights, but perhaps he would want to bid her good-night. And what would he see?

Mary's face looked unnaturally pale above the yellowed linen collar of the nightdress, and she pinched her cheeks. Then there was her hair, still done up in its usual severe knot. She quickly removed the pins; ah, that was better! Her blonde tresses cascaded down her back, reaching to her waist. She still didn't look like a bride waiting to receive her husband, but she wasn't striving for that effect. She merely wanted to present a—yes, she would admit it—a prettier appearance than usual.

She was still staring into her own dark eyes, wondering if her pallor was the fault of the dreadful English climate or her diet, as Mama used to claim, when there was a tap at the door which connected with the sitting room.

"Enter!" said Mary loudly. She sprang away from the mirror, willing her knees not to quiver. It was not necessarily Ramirez; it could be a maid come to warm the bed. Mary had had no such amenities in her old room on the upper floor, but she was in the Queen's Chamber now.

It was Ramirez who came into the room; a disconcerting, even more attractive Ramirez dressed in a dark silk dressing gown and, from what Mary's one shocked glance could tell, nothing else but a pair of slippers. He approached her and had caught both her hands before she could follow her natural instinct to retreat.

"Don't be afraid, my dear, I come only to talk. May I say you're lovely with your hair down?"

Mary was instantly on her guard. She had hoped he would say, or think, something of the kind, but had he only guessed her wishes? Was he flattering her? He must be; she who had never before been called lovely by any human creature save her mother, couldn't inspire that sort of *honest* admiration from such a man.

"*Señor,* please don't," she muttered in a gruff tone.

"My dear, don't you think you could call me Antonio? We are married."

Mary sighed. "Well, you must call me Mary, but we aren't really married. I mean," she added hastily, recalling that the clergyman had indeed said words over them, and that they had made the proper responses, "we are, but we've agreed not to do anything about it—oh, dear." Mary turned quite red; had she still been looking into the mirror, she would have rejoiced that a high colour was quite becoming to her. Ramirez still held her hands. She looked up into his eyes and noticed that kindness was shining from their dark depths. "You didn't come in here to—"

"To rob you of your virtue?" Ramirez smiled, kissed her hands, and released them. "No, indeed. I came in merely to assure you of my continued celibacy. Perhaps I could be your knight, riding hither and yon to do great deeds in your honour, yet never asking for so much as a kiss."

Mary could detect the influence of Don Quixote's favourite characters of chivalry, tales she had enjoyed as a little girl and still dreamed over in secret from time to time. She had never heard anyone in real life talk in so extravagant a manner and knew it must be a joke. In spite of her wish to remain distant, she smiled.

She had to turn severe almost immediately, though, and make her feelings clear. "Sir—Antonio—you shouldn't talk this way. We've made what is essentially a business arrangement, a marriage of convenience. If I were you I wouldn't find it convenient to be stuck out here at Woodbank Hall, but that is for you to choose. And it's not necessary to offer me flattery. I know I'm not the kind of woman to inspire such talk, and I promise you that I can't be taken in by it."

Ramirez looked at her carefully, as if seeing her for the first time. "You don't want a knight?"

"No," said Mary as sternly as she could.

"The truth is, my dear, you didn't expect to find yourself with a knight at your command. But you have one, like it or not."

Mary was so embarrassed by this statement that she said nothing. She was afraid that her professed dislike of flattery had acted as a challenge to this young man, who must be used to women falling at his feet.

"My dear, you must get to sleep, even if it is in that huge ship of a bed," said Ramirez after a long, intimate moment of silence. "I will leave you."

He seemed to sense that there was more she wanted to say, and he stood and waited politely for a moment while she looked at him in helpless confusion. Finally he made as if to leave the room.

"Wait!" cried Mary.

He turned, his eyes betraying his amusement and something else Mary couldn't quite identify. "Yes?"

"I was wondering if you had a comfortable place to sleep." She was merely trying to be polite, she told herself, and thus she didn't mention that she had inspected his quarters earlier.

"Oh. Yes, a very comfortable dressing room next door, with a narrow bed suitable for the monkish life I expect to lead. Everything in the first style; you must not worry about me, though it's very kind of you." A smile teased the corners of his mouth as he looked her up and down more boldly than he ever had.

Mary dropped her eyes. "Well—if you're sure you'll be warm enough, *señor*."

"Not as warm as I'd like, but no more of that. And did I hear a *'señor'*? Antonio, if you please. As your husband, I command it."

"Antonio," whispered Mary. She wished, suddenly, that they were standing closer together.

"Very good. Now, shall we seal our pact of mutual celibacy, my dear wife?"

This sounded like a sensible suggestion. Mary nodded and held out her hand.

Ramirez ignored the hand and stepped forward. Mary found herself enveloped in his embrace, surrounded by the sensation of rustling silk and linen as his robe was crushed against her maidenly nightgown. She felt the warmth of his skin and finally the touch of his lips. Mary had never kissed anyone before. She wouldn't have thought she would know what to do. But her lips parted naturally beneath his for just an instant, and then she pulled away.

"Was that a pact of celibacy?" she enquired with a shaky laugh, looking at the floor. She could feel the colour flooding her face again.

"This *is* our wedding night, is it not?" was Ramirez's enigmatic answer. He kissed her forehead, turned her face up to meet his for one more brief touch of the lips, and then he was gone.

Mary spent her wedding night, as was appropriate, in the arms of her husband. The only singular thing was that the whole passionate encounter took place in her thoughts.

CHAPTER EIGHT

"YOU'RE QUITE CERTAIN." Annabella's voice was urgent; her eyes seemed to bore into the servant girl's rabbity face, gauging the creature's honesty. It was all very well to bribe the staff for information, but how could one trust someone with so little character to have the facts straight?

"Sure as I live, Miss Winter, ma'am," said the chambermaid, bobbing a curtsey. "Them sheets ain't been used for nothing but sleeping on. By one lady."

"Thank you, Jenny. You may go."

The maid curtsied again, picked up the cracked chamber pot which had been her nominal reason for visiting the young lady's room, and which Annabella had cracked on purpose, and went about her duties.

Annabella sat in the middle of her ornate bed, grinning. So cousin Mary hadn't become a woman on her wedding night.

"I knew such a man couldn't marry that little mouse for that reason," she said with satisfaction. A frown creased her broad brow. "The only trouble is—why *did* he do it?"

This question Annabella couldn't answer by chatting with any servant in the house, and she soon decided that the best way to content her curiosity would be to gain Ramirez's confidence herself. Once he was in Annabella's power, who knew what secrets he might divulge? The poor boy must have some deep, dark reason for marrying Annabella's plain cousin, and Annabella knew all the most pleasant ways to find out what it was.

Thus determined, Annabella rose from the bed in a flutter of ruffles, rang for her maid, and proceeded to deck herself out in her best morning costume.

A mere forty-five minutes later, the young lady was descending to the breakfast room. As happened about half the time, the majesty of Annabella's progress down the stairs was marred when she forgot about the historic dog gates on the landing and nearly tripped over them. Disdainfully, she left them open.

In the hall she asked if Count Ramirez were still abed.

The butler informed his young mistress that the foreign gentleman had ridden into London at an early hour. Something about a fencing lesson, Shaldon added, his lip curling in distaste.

"Extraordinary," responded Annabella evenly, but her expression revealed her displeasure. How could Ramirez go out for the day, leaving her in this elaborate outfit with no one to admire it? Because she was hungry, she decided to go in to breakfast, anyway.

The hour was late; Annabella's parents had long since finished and gone about the business of their day. The only inhabitant of the room was Mary.

"You look pale and drawn this morning, dear," said Annabella, moving down the sideboard to fill a plate with a healthy helping of every delicacy available. "Oh, bother! This stuff is cold."

"No one expected you," Mary said, ignoring the comment about her appearance. "Don't you always breakfast in bed?"

"On the morning after my dear cousin's wedding? How shabby that would be." Annabella came to rest in a chair opposite Mary. "Where is your husband?"

"I don't know." Mary saw no reason to equivocate. She didn't expect that she and Ramirez would keep track of each other's movements, and she was about to say as much when Annabella gave a wry chuckle.

"*I* know," she said. "He's gone into London to give a fencing lesson." There was a pause as this sank in; Mary looked vaguely displeased, and Annabella thought gleefully that the ploy had worked. Cousin Mary believed Ramirez had confided in her, Annabella! It was a start.

"Oh," Mary replied. She shrugged. "He did say that he'd continue to earn his living." She wished, for just a moment, that she'd got out of bed at her usual early hour. She might have been able to see her new husband before he left for London.

But she had been awakened, an hour later than her usual time, by the sound of Jenny the chambermaid dropping something heavy. The maid sweetly apologized for waking "Miss—Madam—milady," but she scurried to do the bed as soon as Mary was out of it, leading the new Countess de Ramirez to suppose that Jenny was as inexperienced a servant as she was a bride.

Mary knew that if it hadn't been for the maid's interruption she would have slept on for hours, for she hadn't dropped off until dawn. Tossing and turning, thinking of her first kiss and the disturbing fact that the young man who had kissed her lay in the next room, married to her, Mary had passed a long and wakeful night. What on earth was she to do about Ramirez, or Antonio, as he wanted her to call him? Was it possible? Given her own infatuation and his apparent willingness, could two strangers eventually build a real marriage?

Mary glanced across the table at Annabella. The other girl was bedecked in a cherry-coloured gown more suitable for a special occasion than a boring morning at home. Mary had to admire the rows of lace which formed a ruff at the neck, but she wouldn't have chosen such a fussy costume, especially if her figure were as full as Annabella's. There were too many rosettes on the sleeves, too many ruchings and ribbon knots at the hem as Annabella swished by—altogether a tasteless ensemble. Mary had to admit that her own taste was motivated largely by envy, for she was in a black merino round dress this morning, and she knew the seat was shiny from hard use.

A little prickle, this time of jealousy, went through her as she reflected that Annabella, dressed in that pretty gown, no doubt, had only this morning been receiving Ramirez's confidences! The chit would be up with the birds every day now that there was someone to flirt with in the house. Well, let them play their little games. Mary was above all that.

"You know," said Annabella, talking through her food as she never would have, had there been gentlemen present, "I was a bit startled at your marriage, dear, but now that I've had time to think I've come to realize it's a very good thing."

"Oh?" Mary broke her last piece of toast, waiting.

"Why, yes. For one thing, now there's no need for you to come out socially. Mama was going to push you to find a husband, but now you already have a husband. Mama said yesterday that you and Ramirez should be seen in company, but she wasn't really *thinking*. Why call attention to your, er, unusual marriage? Much better this way. You can remain quietly here, and your husband can go about his business, and we can all be comfortable."

Especially you, thought Mary. Annabella wanted nothing to take the shine out of her own appearance this winter, and an exotic pair of newlyweds, even if the bride was plain, would certainly draw a little attention away from a mere Miss Winter. Try though Mary's cousin might to be significant, in the end she was only a baronet's daughter, one more unmarried girl among droves.

Mary's heart lifted as it occurred to her that she herself was no longer in that unenviable position. If she made her appearance on Ramirez's arm she might not be admired for her beauty, but she would certainly never be ignored.

"Have you had second thoughts about lending me your garnets?" Annabella was asking casually. "Really, Mary, you have a husband already, and you can't blame me for wanting to look my best to attach a suitable gentleman. Do say I can wear them to the hunt ball!''

Mary's voice was extremely sweet as she said, ''I don't lend my garnets, Cousin.'' Annabella was like a dog with a bone! Once she had a wish, nothing would make it go out of her mind but seeing it fulfilled. And this was one wish of Annabella's which wouldn't be, Mary thought, enjoying the displeasure in her cousin's expressive face.

A florid colouring like Annabella's really had no business to be draped in cherry.

IT WAS LATE AFTERNOON before word was brought to Mary that her father was awake and asking for her. She hurried to his chamber straight from the kennels, where she and Lady Winter had been playing with a litter of pups.

Captain Winter was propped up on pillows and looked quite alert, though still wan. ''You didn't ruin yourself last night, my girl, and make an annulment impossible?'' were his opening words.

''Papa!'' Mary glanced at the footman who was just shutting the door behind him and had doubtless heard every embarrassing word. ''I'm glad you're feeling better.''

''Answer me, Daughter!''

''May I remind you, Papa, I told you yesterday that Ramirez and I agreed upon a platonic marriage and, while it is none of your affair, to ease your mind, I will tell you that it has remained so,'' said Mary, feeling herself colour up at the memory of the kiss that had sealed their pact. This annoying new tendency to blush would have to be curbed.

"That's something, at least," said Captain Winter with a relieved sigh. "Now, Mary, you're to listen and listen carefully. I was upset when I learned you'd married."

"I should say so, Papa! The doctor says you've set yourself back at least a week, though I must tell you that he found the brandy bottles under your bed and said it wasn't any wonder that a shocking piece of news had overcome you. You should only be taking watered wine until you're well, you know."

Captain Winter looked exasperated. "Stop changing the subject, girl. I try to warn you and you spout off nonsense about brandy bottles. Must have been the maids leaving 'em under the bed; never could trust an English servant."

"You want to warn me, Papa?"

"That cove Ramirez, Mary, is...well, he ain't what he appears to be."

"He isn't? But he's really a count, Papa; Lord Holland vouched for him." Now, at last, they would come to the reason behind Papa's dreadful reaction to the marriage. Mary waited with the appearance of patience, but she was really as nervous as she had ever been.

The captain scowled before answering grimly. "I'm not saying he ain't from one of the oldest families in Castile. He's a count, all right. That don't mean he's not playing a deep game."

"What sort of game, Papa?" Mary was annoyed. Rather than concrete information, Captain Winter was relying on vagueness and veiled warnings. She was beginning to believe he had nothing against Ramirez at all save for a parental prejudice against an indigent fencing master.

"Maybe I don't know what kind of game yet, but I'll find out," said Captain Winter, neatly confirming Mary's suspicions that he had no specific reason. "Keep your valuables out of his sight, whatever you do. Your mama's necklace especially."

"My necklace!" Mary cried. "Papa, you have said some hurtful things about my husband, but I can't believe you'd ever suspect him of being a common jewel thief. And you know I always keep the necklace safe as a matter of course."

"Good," said the captain. "Now see that he don't cozen you into believing whatever he says. He could charm the necklace away from you before you know where you are. Remember what I've taught you. Men ain't to be trusted. I ought to know, I'm one of 'em."

Mary sighed. No one knew better than she that her father's teachings had indeed taken root. She didn't remember trusting many people in her life, and certainly not a man. She supposed Papa's excessive warnings had been meant for her safety, because she was a young woman living in an uncertain situation. Doña Inez had tried to counteract her husband's safeguarding of their daughter by reminding Mary that many people did have sterling motives, but that lesson had not been demonstrated as well over the years as Captain Winter's advice to "trust no one."

"You really aren't going to explain your aversion to him, are you, Papa," she said resentfully. "You have no right to tell me to distrust Ramirez, to keep my valuables out of his sight, no less, without telling me why."

But Captain Winter's head had disappeared beneath the counterpane. Mary directed a few more comments to the satin quilt, but she had to accept that the interview was over when she heard her father's muffled snores.

She was convinced that her father could have nothing against Antonio. Despite, or perhaps because of, Captain Winter's warning, she resolved to give the man she had married all the trust that would be due to a husband in more traditional circumstances.

WHEN SHE WAS DRESSING for dinner that evening, Mary had a sudden fancy to look at her garnet necklace; it had come into conversations so often lately. She kept the small silk envelope containing her few jewels in the bottom of her workbasket. Spreading a scrap of white silk on the scarlet counterpane of the Queen's bed, she dumped the contents of the envelope onto it. A small jumble of eardrops, bead bracelets, and other trinkets surrounded the evident prize of the collection.

The ruddy, winking stones of the garnet necklace, graduated in size from small to very large, were set in ornate gold. The clasp was a massive, squarish box-catch which boasted its own large garnet, surrounded by tiny pearls. Mary caught the jewels up in her hands, remembering how lovely her mother had looked in this necklace and a regal Court dress. It had been hard to remember, when the necklace was round Mama's throat, that garnets were only semiprecious stones and that the major value of this piece was that of an heirloom. The family of La Rosa had possessed it since the sixteenth century.

Mary couldn't wear it; the garnets clashed badly with her lavender muslin evening gown and would look absurd worn with her more sober dresses. But she clasped the necklace around her neck, testing the stones' effect with her colouring in the mirror set into the wardrobe across from the bed. How could this necklace provoke so much concern? Why did there seem to be a mystery surrounding it?

Mary had asked Mama that very question. "It is better you don't know, Daughter," Doña Inez had replied, a faraway look in her eyes. "You will be told one day, though. Someone will come to you and tell you. Until that time, see you keep the necklace safe."

And though Mary had been puzzled, she had promised easily. She usually didn't think about the necklace from day to day, but recent events made her wonder once more what her mother had meant.

Mary jumped at the sound of her door banging open. Annabella, in an elaborate dressing gown, came into the room.

"Oh!" she said, upon seeing Mary. "I thought sure you'd already be in the drawing room, Cousin, and I wanted to borrow...a bit of ribbon. No, don't stir, I know where it is." Annabella crossed to the dressing table, opened the drawer where Mary kept some trifles, and plucked out a length of velvet ribbon, seemingly at random. "Thank you so much."

Mary stared. She had not yet got used to her cousin's freedom with her possessions. It was not as though they were sisters.

Annabella, on the point of flouncing out of the room, happened to take a good look at Mary. Her gaze fixed on her cousin's throat. "Oh! There is the necklace."

Mary's hand flew to the garnets; she should have had the wit to bundle them away the instant Annabella had come in.

Annabella ran to the bedside and put out her plump hand to touch the stones. Mary shrank back, but not in time. Annabella's fingers closed on the necklace, and she stroked it greedily.

"Oh, I do admire this so much. Please, Cousin. May I try it on?"

"I . . ." Mary had no reason to refuse such an innocent request, which she knew was motivated by harmless vanity. She wanted to refuse it, though. "Those pearls you're wearing might mar the effect," she said, "and I was about to put this away."

"Bother the pearls! May I try the garnets? Please?"

Mary gave the necklace over and watched warily while her cousin preened before the room's largest looking glass. The garnets appeared somehow cheap when worn over a lustrous double rope of pearls. Mary was encouraged to see that the stones did not set off Annabella's complexion to best advantage.

"I'll put the necklace away now, if you don't mind," she said after a few tense moments.

Annabella reluctantly gave back the garnets and began to wander about the room. "You'll put them in your jewel case, I daresay,'' she remarked, her eyes straying to the little pile of trinkets laid out upon the bed. "One can't be too careful with so many precious pieces."

Mary didn't bother to answer this taunt. Neither did she put away her jewellery until Annabella had finally left the room.

"Silly thing," grumbled Mary when she had hidden the silk envelope in another, safer place. "That's the only time you'll ever wear my necklace."

Ramirez was in the corridor when Mary left her bedroom some time later. She started at the sight of him.

He had been surveying a grim portrait of a Winter ancestor, but his eyes lit up when he saw Mary.

"Ah! There you are. I was about to knock, but I didn't want to startle you. Shall we go down?"

Mary nodded. "You were waiting for me?" she asked, flattered that he should have bothered.

"Of course. Shouldn't we appear as a united couple? It's the day after our wedding, you know."

In that same intimate tone of voice had he informed her, the night before, that it was their wedding night—just before he had kissed her. Mary struggled to control her wandering thoughts and took his arm as calmly as she could.

"Antonio," she said as they walked downstairs, her tongue stumbling only a little over his Christian name, "do you think you'll like it here? Or would you prefer to move back to London?"

He grinned. "I hardly think your aunt would be agreeable to your taking up lodgings in the Albany."

"I—I didn't mean me."

"Mary! You would desert me already?"

He halted on the stairs and pressed his free hand to his heart in a consciously dramatic way. Mary laughed and squeezed the arm she held. "Sir, you're incorrigible. I know you went to London today—" *though I didn't hear it from you,* she added silently "—and I simply thought that if you mean to make many such trips—"

"The distance is nothing. Your aunt was kind enough to lend me a prime goer, as she terms him, and I rode into town like the wind. A friend has borrowed my own horse, but he should be returned to me soon, and then I won't have to take the delightful woman's charity. In the matter of her stables, at the least," he added with a shrug.

"You do plan to be away most days?"

"Not most. Two or three times a week I have a full day of classes. My man Jaime is holding the studio open in the Albany, as usual, for the gentlemen's practice. I shall arrange my lessons around your convenience, my dear. Do you want me with you more?"

Mary didn't know what to say in response to this. They entered the drawing room, which luckily made an answer unnecessary.

The ladies of the house were seated in front of a roaring fire. Both looked elegant enough for a company dinner, though this evening there was to be only family. Mary wondered if the ladies' finery was inspired by the exotic young man who had come to live in their midst. She wished that her own lavender gown were more special.

Aunt Winter's dark green silk spread about her in an elegant sweep which ended in the huge, fuzzy mass of Mack, the sheepdog, curled at her feet. Annabella was garbed in a low-necked gown of robin's-egg blue. The two were in the middle of an argument which Mary could hear was about Annabella's habit of leaving the dog gates open. The house spaniels had spent the day in Sir Egbert's library and were now banished to the kennels, to Lady Winter's distress.

"Hmmph! As if a lot of dogs need to be anywhere else but the kennels. Besides, I told you, Mama, Jenny must have left the gates open. The girl's as careless as anything; I don't know why you put up with it," Annabella said with a sniff. Then she noticed the newlyweds and turned all her charm on Ramirez.

Mary, summoned by her aunt, couldn't help being dismayed by Annabella's blatant tactics. While Mary murmured nothings about the tenants she would visit for Aunt Winter on the morrow, Annabella drifted over to the pianoforte, and Ramirez followed. Amidst shrill giggles from Annabella and the occasional low murmur from Ramirez, the two looked over the music on top of the instrument.

There came a louder squeal than usual. "Oh, Cousin Tony!" cried Annabella. "I'd be delighted."

Cousin Tony? Mary's head came up sharply.

"Don't look like you're sucking on a lemon, girl, the chit's only showing off," was Lady Winter's sage advice. "You know how she is. The men don't take her seriously, more's the pity. I only hope that St. Charles boy comes up to scratch."

"Cousin... Tony?" Mary muttered, frowning awfully. He had asked her to call him Antonio, and how thrilled she had been to do so. That was before he had given her unbearable cousin the free use of his pet name. Mary set her jaw. It would be a long time before she called him anything but *señor*.

"Do you know something, Mary my child? You're fond of the boy already," said Lady Winter. "I knew how it would be."

"No, Aunt. I'm simply feeling a bit ill," said Mary, reasoning that this was the truth. Few things made her sicker than the sight of Annabella in action, and when Ramirez was the quarry—

"Wait'll he hears her sing," said Lady Winter. "More than one young man has found his heart again. You worry too much, my dear. He married you, didn't he?"

Mary could not contradict this; she reached down to pat Mack and wished she had brought her work to hide behind. She looked so sad that Lady Winter tried to distract her with the promise of another visit to the kennels in the morning.

Meanwhile, Annabella began her song. Mary, who was a good singer herself, didn't have to feel envious of her cousin's high, thin voice, nor her indifferent manner of plunking the occasional key to accompany what she obviously considered one of her greatest assets. Ramirez patiently turned the pages of "Yellow-Haired Laddie," which Mary gathered he had requested, and his manner seemed very attentive from a distance. He leaned solicitously over the keyboard, returning Annabella's smile each time she looked up

from her music—which was rather often. That Annabella lost her place each time she did this, and had
to have it pointed out for her by "dear Cousin Tony,"
did little to lighten Mary's mood.

When Sir Egbert came in, his entrance followed
shortly by the butler's announcement that dinner was
on table, the party reorganized. Lady Winter demanded that Ramirez take his wife in to dinner, and
Annabella was foiled for the moment. Since they were
a family party, Mary's cousin continued to practice
her wiles all through the meal, sending flirtatious
comments and intimate glances across the table like
Cupid's darts.

"For the Lord's sake, let up on the young man until he has a bite to eat," Lady Winter admonished her
daughter at one point, echoing Mary's disgust.

Annabella subsided into stony silence, and Ramirez, to Mary's astonishment, exchanged a knowing
glance with his wife.

"You act as though we're sharing some kind of
joke, sir," she whispered to him carefully.

"Don't you think this is a very good joke indeed?"
was his answer. "Your cousin is an odd young lady."

Odd! Mary felt better than she had all evening. She
sensed that Ramirez hadn't fallen into Annabella's net,
and that was enough for the moment. She would have
liked to take him to task, however, for appearing to
fall in with her cousin's schemes.

Annabella, on seeing the newlyweds exchange
words, magically came out of her sulks and recap-
tured "Cousin Tony's" attention for the rest of the
meal.

When the three ladies and two gentlemen re-grouped later in the drawing room, Ramirez sought out Mary, and she immediately voiced her thoughts. "What do you mean by flirting with my cousin?" she said in a low voice, for Annabella was bearing down upon them already.

"Better ask her what she means by flirting with me," said Ramirez. "I'm a married man." He turned his head slightly to greet Annabella. "Cousin! We're delighted to see you, but I need to talk to my wife."

Annabella's expressive features registered amazement, but she quickly put her simpering mask back on and said, "Indeed! Well, I'll wait for you at the instrument, Cousin Tony. You know I promised to sing to you some more."

Was that a barely perceptible shudder of the broad, black-clad shoulders? wondered Mary, narrowly observing Ramirez's reaction to the prospect of this treat.

"You need to talk to me, sir? What a surprise," she said with a touch of sarcasm. "I would hate to keep you from Annabella's singing. Why don't you run along?"

"I had nothing in particular to discuss, my dear, I simply wished a moment of your company, since it would appear I'm to be enslaved by your cousin yet again."

"Did it never occur to you that you might say no to her?"

"How rude that would be! To her mother as well as to her, and I am a guest in their home. Such is the price of taking charity."

"Well, it's your choice. You may go back to live in London any time you wish, and I won't stop you," said Mary in irritation. She was not satisfied with his explanation in the least. Nothing compelled even the politest guest to flirt back!

Ramirez eyed her with affection, or so it appeared. "My dear, I delight in your jealousy. It gives me hope for the future."

Mary cast down her eyes in anger and embarrassment and said nothing further.

Annabella had apparently decided not to leave her conquest to chance. She bounced back to their corner, hands full of music. "Oh, Cousin Tony, we'd better get on with our little project. It's growing late. Do help me choose which song to sing." She sat herself down right between Mary and Ramirez, and Mary instantly got up.

"Don't go, Mary," said Annabella insincerely, eyes sparkling as they turned on her latest flirt.

"I wouldn't dream of interfering with your 'little project,'" Mary returned as sweetly. She wandered a short distance away and turned over some books on a lowboy, not even seeing the titles as she blatantly eavesdropped on the pair's conversation.

"You haven't even told me how you like my new dress," said Annabella in a chiding tone. Whereas some people angled for compliments on their apparel, Annabella cast out a net. She had demanded Antonio's opinion of her costume the night before, Mary remembered.

"Ah! Is it new?" Ramirez's smooth voice seemed to be less than sincere. Mary was becoming surer by the minute that his gallantries to Annabella were motivated only by amusement, with perhaps a dash of ennui. A man of his intelligence couldn't take Mary's cousin seriously. He himself had called her odd. "A perfect colour for you, my dear, er, Cousin," he said.

"Oh, I must admit there are those who agree with you. Mr. St. Charles says this colour sets off my eyes."

The conversation degenerated into an earnest discussion of Annabella's wardrobe, thus mercifully forestalling the singing of another song, and Mary picked up one of the books in front of her, a volume of poetry. But she could not have told if the verses were by Pope or Shakespeare, for she was fighting to keep back an attack of the very jealousy Ramirez had taunted her with, and which she disdained to admit to herself.

Shaldon, the butler, bowed before her. He held a silver salver with a folded note upon it. "For you, madam. It was just delivered."

Mary took the letter in amazement. Never had a message been delivered to her in her uncle's house. "Miss Winter" was the direction on the outside, and Mary broke the plain seal and unfolded the paper immediately.

Someone with a rangy scrawl had written, *I long to see you. I think you know why.* There was a signature, and Mary's eyes boggled as she read, *St. Charles.* Annabella's beau!

The butler had already left the room. Mary had once heard Shaldon arguing with the housekeeper over who was "Miss Winter" now that there were two young ladies of the same surname in the house: Mary, because she was the elder, or Annabella, because she was the daughter of Sir Egbert. The servants had appealed to Mary, but she hadn't known what to tell them. It had obviously slipped Shaldon's mind that Captain Winter's daughter now had quite another title, and that the confusion should be over.

Mary considered for a moment that the note might be meant for her. Hadn't Mr. St. Charles addressed her as "Miss Winter" on the day that she'd been married? And hadn't he flirted rather outrageously with her for some unknown reason? However, she was reminded how Antonio had put a definite period to Mr. St. Charles's attentions and doubted very much whether that man would ever consider empty gallantries again. No, she was certain Mr. St. Charles had intended the note for Annabella, and what was more, it appeared as if he intended to advance his suit.

Now what was she to do? It wasn't proper for Annabella to receive suggestive notes from men. Mary might confront her cousin and risk a scene, or she might give the note to her aunt and become that most contemptible of creatures, a tale-bearer.

Or she might talk to St. Charles at the next opportunity and warn him not to arrange clandestine meetings with Annabella. Though the thought of doing any such thing made Mary shudder, she decided the last was the most practical course and determined to follow it, as soon as circumstances threw her in Mr. St. Charles's way.

CHAPTER NINE

MUCH TIME WAS TO PASS before Mary was able to keep her resolution to act as her cousin's duenna and warn Mr. St. Charles against leading Annabella astray.

Meanwhile she was getting used to her strange new status as a married woman. Not that her daily life was changed in any great particular: she still cared for her father, whose condition slowly improved after one relapse into the fever, and did little commissions for Lady Winter. But reminders of her change in situation did arise now and again. The notice of her marriage appeared in the *Times*, and Mary clipped out the item and placed it with her private papers, although she was too shy to call Antonio's attention to it. Soon after the notice a magnificent silver vase arrived, bearing Lady Holland's card. It was Mary's first wedding present.

Ramirez went into town several days a week to give fencing lessons; or, on the rare occasions he stayed at home, he closeted himself for most of the day with Sir Egbert in the latter gentleman's library. Mary was surprised at this development, but when she questioned Antonio one day, he would only say that he and Sir Egbert found much matter for intelligent discussion.

"But you are right; I am neglecting my wife," he added with a warm smile. "Tomorrow I stay in the country. Why don't we ride together?"

Mary was much flattered by this suggestion and agreed, hoping she didn't sound too eager.

She was ready next day when Ramirez knocked on her door to escort her to the stables. To her disgust, she nearly trembled in anticipation of what the coming interlude might bring.

The newlywed pair had left the house and were approaching the stables through the gardens when they heard the clatter of booted footsteps behind them on the brick walkway. "Naughty Cousin Tony!" sang out Annabella, managing to sound enticing and kittenish, though totally out of breath.

Mary's heart sank as she and her husband turned around.

Annabella's obviously new riding habit, moulded tightly to her figure, was an unusual shade of buff which worked in perfect harmony with her red-gold hair. A large, plumed riding hat of gold velvet set off her costume. Annabella's splendour left Mary feeling more crowlike than usual in her familiar black habit, the garment she had always considered her favourite, and which she had been longing for Antonio to see.

Ramirez didn't act disconcerted or even surprised that his "cousin" had sought them out. "Shall we go, ladies? A perfect day for a ride," he said, offering his free arm to Annabella. "But I'm rather puzzled, dear Cousin. Weren't you telling me only the other day that you'd rather be—how did you put it? Oh, yes—locked in a tower with a pack of lions than go riding with your

mother? Something about hating the sight, smell, and
touch of a horse?''

"Oh, well, you know Mama and I have our little
quarrels," said Annabella, flashing a murderous look
at Mary, who had burst into giggles. "Shall we go?"
Her long eyelashes fluttered about, and she encouraged the dimple at the side of her mouth.

Mary maintained a pleasant expression, but her
merriment of a moment before was gone the way of
her precious tête-à-tête with Antonio.

The three were soon mounted. Ramirez now had his
own horse, returned to him by the friend who had
borrowed it. Amadís was a massive black stallion,
quite the sort of beast Mary pictured her husband
would own. She secretly thought that when he was
mounted Antonio resembled a knight out of Spanish
legend. Mary used her aunt's second-favourite hunter, a spirited grey, and Annabella took out her personal horse, a red-gold mare more sluggish than
anything else in the stables but quite suited to Miss
Winter's negligible riding abilities. Mary suspected her
cousin had chosen Strawberry in the first place to
complement her hair, disregarding such things as wind
and gait. Aunt Winter had the final say on every horse
in her stable, however, and Strawberry was overfed
and underridden, but nothing worse.

"Do let's go into the village," suggested Annabella
brightly when they were all trotting through the gates
of Woodbank Hall. "It's such a lovely day."

Mary sighed. The day was indeed fine: clear, cold,
magnificent riding weather, the sort of weather that
made one long for a canter or even a gallop across the

fields, not a sedate trip into the same village one visited on foot every other day. Not the least of Annabella's disadvantages as a riding companion was her tendency to limit her exercise to the tame and boring.

Glancing at Ramirez, Mary thought she intercepted a look of vexation from his slanting dark eyes; but his words were gracious as ever as he agreed to Annabella's plan.

The village was not a mile distant. The party was there in no time despite Annabella's tendency to poke about and let Strawberry nuzzle at all the dead weeds. Mary sat her horse gloomily, listening to Annabella flirt and Ramirez, to do him credit, parry the delicate thrusts.

"Oh, we must get down and walk a bit," cried Annabella when they reached the first cottage in the little settlement. "I'm so dreadfully tired."

Tired? Mary shook her head. She longed to snap at the girl that no one could be tired from such a short and desultory ride, but she knew Ramirez would not do so, and she hated to be less gracious than her husband. She let Antonio help her dismount, enjoying the feel of his hands round her middle and exulting in the fact that he helped her first. She could even survey with a tolerable equanimity the way Annabella writhed and squealed in his grasp as he next jumped his fair cousin down from her mount.

Once they were all on the ground and had tethered their horses to the wicket fence of the first cottage, the trio moved through the village. Annabella said she had to stop at the church to see if the flowers she had sent over had been properly placed. Mary, who knew that

Annabella had never done any church or village business in her life, wondered why the girl didn't simply
admit that the flowers, like the flowers the church had
every week, were sent from the Woodbank Hall con-
servatories on Lady Winter's standing order. Annabella was doubtless trying to show Ramirez what a
sweet, domestic little thing she was.

Well, at least the village was pleasant, and Mary was
on one of her handsome husband's arms, even if the
chattering and simpering Annabella was clinging to
the other. Mary could take real pleasure in looking
about at the neat, thatched cottages, gardens stripped
and battened down for winter; and the weathered
stone church, with its one soaring spire, reminded her
of pictures she had seen and admired of Salisbury
Cathedral. After so many years abroad, Mary could
appreciate the Englishness of the village on its own
account, almost as a foreign tourist might.

Annabella led the way into the church, ascertained
with a nod of her head that the flowers were there, and
immediately turned round again. She suggested a stroll
to look at the gravestones.

"My dear Cousin," Ramirez said, giving Annabella an odd look, "the day is young. We have barely
begun our ride. Could we not wander among the
gravestones some other day?"

Annabella bestowed a charming smile upon him.
"Oh, I only meant to walk and, er, rest for a few minutes more. I simply can't get back on that great big
horse quite yet." With a pleading glance, she turned
the situation to her own account. "But I would be delighted to bring you back here at any time, Cousin

Tony, and we shall have a nice, leisurely tour of the churchyard. The vicar has told me many old stories that I'm sure would interest you." Her eyes took on a heavy-lidded look which anyone but an idiot must recognize as a hint that more than stories of bygone villagers would await the lucky man to walk with Annabella in the churchyard.

Mary could see that Ramirez looked more amused than intrigued, but she could also tell that Annabella hadn't sensed this and considered "Cousin Tony" quite in her trap. Her husband's infernal politeness to Annabella drove Mary to turn her back before she could say something cutting. As she gazed over the gravestones to the field beyond, which had a footpath connecting it to the churchyard, she noticed a man approaching.

He drew nearer, and Mary saw that he was big, blonde, and handsome. Mr. St. Charles! He doffed his hat and waved.

Mary wondered if this meeting could have been prearranged despite her own mistaken interception of St. Charles's note to Annabella.

If the man had arranged to meet Annabella, he certainly gave no sign of any such intrigue. His face was all honest surprise and delight.

"Oh, Mr. St. Charles!" Annabella was even more surprised than the young man; suspiciously so, Mary thought. "I'm sure you remember my cousins."

"Actually, Mr. St. Charles and I were not introduced," Ramirez said with a bow.

Annabella performed the duty quickly. "Do you remember, Cousin Tony, I told you of Mr. St.

Charles? He lost his way during the last hunt and ended up on our property, miles from the fox, and I happened to be out . . ."

Mary lost interest in this recitation of Annabella's conquest, and her mind wandered. Let the gentlemen do the polite and act as her cousin's audience. Mary began to wonder if she could decently leave the group and continue her ride by herself. She was longing for more air and exercise than was likely as long as Annabella made one of the party.

Mary came out of her reverie to find St. Charles gripping her gloved hand.

"Lady Ramirez, I'm delighted to see you again," he said. "Shall we walk a bit?"

Annabella's mouth fell open, Ramirez's eyebrows shot upward, and Mary said, "What?" in a blank voice.

St. Charles tried again. "Walk around the churchyard, don't you know. All of us have been riding; we could use to stretch the legs."

Annabella grabbed Ramirez's arm and said, "An excellent idea, Mr. St. Charles. Perhaps you two can catch us up." She nearly pulled "Cousin Tony" down the path leading to the more imposing family sepulchres.

St. Charles was smiling widely, and his eyes were sparkling, as he offered his arm to Mary.

She accepted it, realizing that this was a golden opportunity to deliver the message about his activities with Annabella. She took a deep breath. "Sir, I ought to tell you that by mistake your note to Annabella of a few days ago was delivered to me." She hesitated, not knowing quite how to phrase the warning that must follow. The two of them were strolling behind Annabella and Ramirez, and Mary slowed her steps so as not to embarrass St. Charles before the others.

Her companion's neck was not visible due to his extremely high shirt points, but Mary was certain that it would be as red as his ears had turned. "Ma'am, I—what can I say? It wasn't anything improper, as you know."

Mary hated to be compelled to play the duenna, but what else could she do? "I feel it only right to warn you, sir, that you must not see Annabella alone. I might be a little stiff in these matters because I lived on the Peninsula for so long, but I know that my cousin's independent streak mustn't be encouraged. Her reputation is at stake." She realized in passing how odd it was for her, of all people, whose reputation had died that fateful morning at Tattersall's, to be playing the strict guardian of her heedless cousin.

Mr. St. Charles luckily took no offense. "A man must bow to such a sentiment, but I assure you, ma'am, I mean nothing but respect to Miss Winter. And now let's turn the subject. Will you save me a dance at the hunt ball? To forward our acquaintance, don't you know."

Mary understood that he was trying to distract her from the subject of his conduct with Annabella. "I can't promise, sir," she said repressively. "And I'm not certain I'll be attending the hunt ball." She had no idea whether she and Ramirez would even be invited; callers had been conspicuously absent at the Hall in the past days, and Mary surmised that this was because the scandal of her marriage day had spread throughout the neighbourhood.

"Not go to the ball!" exclaimed the young man, too loudly, for Annabella and Ramirez turned round to stare.

Annabella said, "Mary doesn't like to go out, you know, Mr. St. Charles. It's no use to expect her to attend the ball."

"We must nip this shyness of my wife's in the bud," said Ramirez, smiling at Mary. "You must have been asking for a dance, sir. My lady will be delighted to grant you one."

"And I shall be delighted to grant *you* one, Cousin Tony," Annabella said quickly. She looked hard at St. Charles.

"And may I have your first dance, Miss Winter?" the young man requested after only a moment of uncomfortable silence.

"You may, if Cousin Tony is able to spare me."

"All of which will depend on whether or not we go to the hunt ball," said Mary curtly. "I haven't heard."

"Ah, yes, the scandal. That might make a difference." Ramirez appealed to St. Charles. "Do you think Lord Burnham will let the odd circumstance of our marriage weigh with him, sir? Perhaps you could cajole him, since you are staying with him and wish so ardently to dance with my wife."

"Quite so. I'll do my best," said St. Charles heartily. "Don't forget, then, Lady Ramirez. Husband's approval and all that. Do I have your promise?"

Annabella was looking stormy; even Ramirez's good humour seemed to be shifting to a jealous frown.

"Naturally I'll dance with you, sir, if I have the occasion," Mary said in a neutral tone.

Annabella saved the situation for herself by leaving Ramirez, attaching herself to St. Charles, and demanding to be taken to see his new horse, which he'd told her so much about. The young man easily let himself be borne away.

"My dear, you might find yourself in dangerous waters there," said Ramirez with an admonishing shake of his head, when he and Mary were alone.

Mary glared at him. "He simply asked for a dance. As it happens, I was taking him to task for writing notes to Annabella. You can't blame me for playing the duenna."

"He's been writing her notes? They are betrothed?" Antonio spoke sharply.

Mary shook her head and explained that a note for Annabella had been mistakenly given to her.

"You were right to speak to him, then." He hesitated. "What did the note say?"

"It was only a silly little private message, and I shouldn't have told you as much as I did."

Antonio looked worried, and Mary was piqued that he would show so much concern for Annabella.

Annabella and St. Charles came back into view then, and all chance for private conversation ceased. Annabella looked mollified, and St. Charles satisfied, as only a successful suitor could be. He had doubtless made some excuse to Annabella for asking Mary for a dance. He decided to accompany the riders back to Woodbank Hall and was careful that he and his sturdy roan hunter never strayed too far from Annabella and Strawberry.

Mary and Ramirez rode side by side. The distance back to the Hall from the village seemed absurdly short, and Mary was irritated that they should have no better chance for exercise.

"You, my sweet Mary, are the classic case of a female who has not had enough chance to test her powers," said Ramirez in a conversational tone as the party turned in at the gates of the estate.

Mary nearly laughed. "I have no idea what you mean."

"Certainly you do. You need attentions not only from me and this St. Charles, but from other men as well. You have not had enough time out in society; this makes you tend to discount my admiration rather than accept it as your due. You must definitely attend this hunt ball."

"You forget I'm a scandalous woman," said Mary. His words embarrassed her, and she sought to change the subject. The four took the side path round to the stables. "Lord Burnham will doubtless think hard before he invites either you or me, thanks to that morning in Tattersall's."

"I have a feeling that if there is any question, Mr. St. Charles will beg in your—our—favour." Ramirez looked wise.

Mary wanted to say something very severe, but she couldn't. St. Charles had dismounted and was standing beside her, offering to jump her down.

"Don't be afraid, Lady Ramirez," said the young man, his broad face alight, "I'll make his lordship see reason if there's any talk of not inviting you." He gave her a nod and definitely squeezed her waist too hard as he helped her to dismount.

Mary thought it best not to notice. St. Charles might want to play an empty game with a safely married woman, but she did not have to join in.

She tried very hard not to triumph in the situation when Annabella was particularly cold to her for the rest of the day, and desperately coy with "Cousin Tony"—at least in Mary's presence.

RAMIREZ MENTIONED THE BALL to Lady Winter that very afternoon in the drawing room, and her ladyship ordered the newly married pair to attend. "Your first appearance as man and wife. Can't let it go by without a little flourish or two. I'll give a party for you here later, but I hate balls, and there ain't nothing like a dancing party for a grand entrance."

Annabella was present, and she was quick to object. "Not only might Lord Burnham not invite them, but Mary has nothing to wear, Mama, and it's too late to have something made."

"Fustian! I sent her measurements to London the day after her wedding and ordered her a nice gown. It arrived this very day. A little wedding present, my dear." She turned to Mary, who smiled and murmured her thanks. "You should find the box on your bed by now. Meant it for a surprise. As for Lord Burnham, I'll handle that one if there's any chance he's so foolish as to slight my young relations."

Annabella let out her breath in a rush and crossed the room to the harp, another of the instruments she had pretended to study. Under cover of some angry-sounding twanging, Lady Winter informed Mary and Ramirez that the gown would help Mary put Anna-bella in the shade.

But Mary knew that no matter how elegant her gown, she could never draw attention from Anna-bella. Her cousin in the full glory of evening dress would make Mary seem a pale moon next to the blazing sun.

Unable to concentrate on her work or a book, thanks to the thought of new finery upstairs, Mary excused herself before long. Her aunt indulgently let her go while Annabella glared.

To Mary's surprise, Ramirez went with her to her room. "I wish to see this ball gown," he said with a wink, opening the door to her chamber as though they were about to retire together. "Then I'll leave you to try it on."

"How odd that you should be curious! I mean—you're a man."

"Thank you for noticing. And why should it be odd that I take an interest in everything concerning you? I have hopes that this will be something to do you justice. Though you look lovely in your mourning clothes, the time for them is long past."

Mary managed to hold back her astonishment that he had actually been noticing her wardrobe.

On the high bed sat a very large white box tied up with a red ribbon. Mary opened it quickly, pushed aside some silver paper, and drew out a lustrous mass of garnet-coloured silk.

"My goodness!" she cried. Her first thought was that she, so pale and drab, would disappear if she wore such a bright, jewellike colour. She realized that her aunt had remembered the garnet necklace and ordered the dress to match it. And Lady Winter wanted Mary to cut a dash; a quiet colour was out of the question. But Mary had never worn evening clothes in anything but white and the palest pinks and blues before going into mourning. She doubted if she could appear in such a gown; she was too shy. And wasn't this a colour more suitable for an older woman?

Ramirez saw the uncertainty and displeasure on her face. Gently he took the gown from her hands and shook it out. "Perfect," he pronounced, holding it up in front of her. "A gown fit for a countess of Spain."

Mary had to agree that the gown was no dowager's. When it was held up she could tell that the style was graceful, an artfully draped tunic over a sinuous underskirt, all in shimmering lustring. The neck appeared to be extremely low. But would her blonde hair show to advantage? And her pale skin?

"Take it to the mirror," said Ramirez. He seemed to be reading her thoughts. "And I'll leave you to preen in privacy. That colour will become you, my dear." Pressing a kiss on her forehead, he left the room.

Mary shivered at the kiss, but the gown was uppermost in her mind. She waited only a moment after the door closed behind Ramirez before racing to the mirror, her new dress held up to her face. It was true! Thanks, perhaps, to her dark eyes and skin of a tone more commonly seen on a dark-haired lady, the garnet silk made her glow. Bless Aunt Winter!

Still, the prospect of wearing the gown to a ball, entering a room full of curious people after being announced as "Lady Ramirez" filled Mary with nothing so much as dread.

CHAPTER TEN

MARY SMILED, first at her reflection in the dark-framed cheval glass and then at the portrait of the red-haired queen above the bedroom mantelpiece. Queen Elizabeth, with her love of bright colours, might well have delighted in such a gown as this had she been alive in the present day. Good Queen Bess would think it a shame, though, for a lady to be dressed so gaily, so fashionably, without a single bauble at throat or wrists.

"Very nice, milady," was the smug opinion of Lady Winter's dresser. Hobbes, a haughty and well-trained tiring-woman who was not best pleased that her major duty in life was the brushing of dog hairs from her lady's practical riding habits, had been delighted to help the new countess dress for the ball. She had just done Lady Ramirez's hair to perfection in a smooth and gleaming knot, and now she stepped back from hooking the garnet-coloured ball gown. "You do quite right to wear no jewels. The simplicity is striking."

Mary nodded her thanks, touching her bare throat. The dresser might well be correct, but... "That will be all, Hobbes," she said in her best imitation of the titled lady she was always having to remind herself she was. "And thank you for working your miracles with my hair."

Hobbes curtsied and went on her way, and Mary, as soon as she was alone, crossed to the wardrobe, stood on a chair, and drew down from the top of the cabinet the little packet which contained her jewellery. She felt a bit silly safeguarding it as though there were thieves in the house, moving its hiding place from spot to spot, but in order to keep her promise to her mother she felt she must be careful. Annabella had been expressing too much interest in the stones. Mary planned to leave her throat bare tonight and was glad that Hobbes had approved the look. But there was no reason not to test the effect of the garnets with this lovely gown that had been made to set them off.

As soon as the jewels were around her neck, Mary wondered if she should reconsider her decision. The necklace and the gown looked so very well together. Surely it would not matter...

But the prospect of Annabella's snappish mood, should she see the necklace on Mary, soon decided the point. No personal display was worth an evening of her cousin looking daggers and picking quarrels. The garnets were best left at home.

Someone scratched at the door. "Enter!" called Mary.

The maid Jenny peeked her dumpling-shaped head in at the door; a broom appeared beside her. "Oh, your pardon, milady, didn't know you was still in. Hobbes said I was to clean some powder off the carpet."

"She must have mistaken the room. There was nothing spilled here," said Mary, wondering why the girl's eyes would always shift about in that odd way. She had never gotten on with Jenny. "You may go."

Jenny bobbed up and down and shut the door carefully. She had to open it again when her broom caught in it.

Mary shrugged off the incident, but she did hide the garnets in a special new place before she left her room. Much as she hated to distrust her uncle's servants, many of them gave her queer feelings from time to time, from Shaldon with his delivery of notes to the wrong people, to Jenny with her consciously clumsy ways.

Before descending to the drawing room Mary looked in on her father; she had promised to show him her finery before setting off for the evening.

Sitting up in a tattered dressing gown before the fire, Captain Winter was just finishing a meal of boiled chicken and beef jelly. Mary noted with some amusement that the glass of watered wine beside the dinner plate was untouched. He pushed away the small table and regarded his daughter. "Thank the Lord you've sense enough to leave your jewellery off," he said.

Mary had expected some allusion to her becoming costume. She had actually flattered herself that Papa must wish to see her in her ball gown in order to admire her. Instead he was reminding her of his distrust of Antonio. She frowned. "Are you still playing that old tune, Papa?" There was no need to confide in him those misgivings about Annabella which had led her not to wear the necklace. "My husband is perfectly trustworthy."

"That's as may be. Best not to go showing off what you own and make him protest the annulment or some such," Captain Winter muttered.

"I'm not sure there will be an annulment, Papa." Mary spoke the words quietly, surprised at herself for voicing that daring thought. Her admiration for Antonio was growing. He seemed really to admire her in return. It would behoove her to prepare Papa for the possibility that she could well be married for good.

"Foolish chit." Captain Winter scowled, but he didn't argue the point with her. Then his expression softened at last. "You look pretty tonight, Daughter. See you have a care."

Mary flushed with pleasure at the long-awaited compliment and kissed her father's cheek. Smiling, she went down to show herself to the rest of the family.

Annabella was the only person in the drawing room. Reclining upon a sofa, her opulent form clad in white gauze over pale blue satin, she looked quite at her ease. A delicate sapphire set twinkled at her neck and ears. She took one careful look at Mary, taking in her costume from hair to slippers, and shrugged.

Mary hadn't expected more of a reaction from her cousin. Disappointed that Ramirez had not been in the room to behold her entrance in her new gown, she sat down near Annabella. An unusual thrill of satisfaction ran through her all the same. How pleasant to know that for the first time in her life her dress outshone her cousin's.

"Do you like my new gown?" Annabella chattered. "Since Mama bought you *that* I really didn't think it fair that I shouldn't have a new one, too. I spent more on this than on all my quarter's clothes combined because it had to be made up so fast. But don't tell Mama. I get only a hundred a quarter as pin money, you know, but that would not serve to keep me in stockings and fans...."

Lady Winter's entrance brought a merciful end to the topic of how much Annabella had to pay for this and that. Mary's aunt was splendid in purple satin trimmed with silver cord, an elaborate turban surmounting her iron-grey crimps. Her eyes were riveted immediately on Mary. "Niece, I bought you that dress on purpose to show off your Mama's necklace. Where the deuce is it?"

Mary was suddenly as nervous as though she'd stolen the garnets rather than simply decided to keep them out of sight. "Hobbes said that the simplicity of my costume is striking," she began. She would be hard put to explain the uneasiness which had made her forego wearing the necklace.

"Simplicity may fly to the moon! Go and get the necklace, child. This is a night for display." Lady Winter touched her own elaborate collar of amethysts. "I let that silly chit borrow the sapphires," she added with a nod at Annabella.

"I'd really prefer to let this gown stand on its own," Mary said lamely.

"I think she's right, Mama," put in Annabella. Mary's head turned sharply.

"That, er, elaborate dress is enough in itself," Annabella explained. She did not meet Mary's eye.

Lady Winter frowned and looked hard at her niece. "Well, you may be right, young ladies. And Hobbes always is."

Hard on the heels of this decision the drawing-room door opened again, and Ramirez entered, splendid in his familiar dark evening attire. Mary found herself gazing at him quite in the style of an adoring schoolgirl. When he met her eyes she looked quickly down at her lap.

"You look lovely, ladies," he said with a brilliant smile for everyone. "I'll delight in squiring three such beauties." His eyes came to rest again on Mary, who had dared to look up, and she remembered for the first time that evening how very low her new gown was in the bosom. "My dear wife, you are a feast for the eyes. But isn't something missing? Wouldn't this be the night for your most becoming jewels?"

"You, too? I told her she ought to get out her garnets, a very fine piece she has from her mother, but the girl refuses," said Lady Winter. "Ramirez is a man of taste, Mary. Perhaps you'd better go up to your room and put that necklace on."

Ramirez was smiling at Mary expectantly. She smiled back, then addressed her aunt. "I think that I'll leave my costume as it is. I trust your abigail's judgment."

Lady Winter nodded sagely, Ramirez looked confused, and Annabella appeared to be satisfied, quite probably because without jewels Mary would be a lesser rival to her own elegantly clad person. The discussion of Mary's outfit foundered, at last, when Sir Egbert joined the party.

They soon moved to dinner, where Ramirez and Lady Winter made the meal lively with their argument over whether the dance could rival riding as a healthful activity. Ramirez swore to show Lady Winter that it could.

"This very night, Madam," he said suavely. "Be prepared."

The little group was treated to the unusual sight of Letitia Winter blushing like a schoolgirl.

IMMEDIATELY UPON their entrance later that evening into the Palladian front hall of Lord Burnham's mansion, an unusually excited Mr. St. Charles rushed up to the party before they could take off their cloaks, and grasped Mary's hand. "Lady Ramirez! Glad to see you at last. You do remember our dance?"

"My good man, you forget yourself," said Ramirez coldly, stepping between his wife and the large young man. Annabella stared at St. Charles as though he were a candidate for Bedlam. The elder Winters' shocked gazes were riveted on their hitherto quiet niece, Mary.

"Good evening, sir," was Mary's neutral statement, delivered over Ramirez's protective shoulder. St. Charles grinned and fastened on Annabella, which made everyone in the party heave sighs of relief.

Mary concentrated her energies on untying her cloak, giving it to the servant, and entering her first English ball on the arm of her husband, who certainly qualified as the handsomest and most dashing man in this or any other room.

She and Ramirez were the first of their group to go into the ballroom, for Lady Winter insisted that the young couple go on ahead so that they might create more of a stir. Sir Egbert, her ladyship, and a disgruntled Annabella hovered behind "Lord and Lady Ramirez." The press of people, many of whom she had never met, shocked Mary despite her resolution to remain calm at all cost. Every eye seemed turned to her and her husband as they descended a flight of marble steps into the pilastered ballroom.

Then an excited babbel of conversation broke out, and the Winters officially joined the party. Annabella was surrounded by her usual coterie of young men, the elder Winters began to greet their friends, and Mary and Ramirez stood to one side, being introduced, nodding to people they already knew, and feeling, at least in Mary's case, quite uncomfortable. None of these people had paid their usual calls at the Winters' of late, and most looked surprised to see the Ramirez couple there. Mary feared she knew why.

The music struck up just as she was growing desperate to be out of the room. She might be prey to an overactive imagination, but she didn't appear to be receiving the respect due a "Lady Ramirez." People were civil, but they bowed to her in an offhand manner before making a fuss over her husband. Then, one stern matron refused to take Mary's hand. The lady stared straight at it and withdrew her own.

"Our first dance, my dear," said Ramirez, breaking up this last, disturbing incident to lead Mary away from the group. As they walked toward a nearby set of dancers, Mary heard the word "Tattersall's" uttered in a shrill whisper by one of the females she had just met.

"I knew it," she said with a sigh. "The nine days' wonder. They couldn't let the matter be forgotten."

"Yes, Mary? Perhaps my English is not good enough. I don't understand...." Ramirez's dark eyes looked down into hers, questioning the distressed tone in her voice.

"Oh, you know you speak English perfectly. I've been thinking over why those people were so rude to me. No, I shouldn't say rude, it was more coldly civil. The day you and I married is still the talk of the district."

"Is that all?" Ramirez chuckled. "Rather amusing, is it not?"

"It would be if I were you. You're obviously to be treated as the chivalrous hero who was good enough to marry this scandalbound sinner."

"I love your irony, but trust me to scotch any such talk."

"But it won't reach your ears! It's simply a difference in the depth of a bow, a hand refused—that sort of thing. Annabella was right all along. I *do* hate society," said Mary, rather too loudly. A head or two turned at these strong words.

"Shh! Here is a set with room for us," said Ramirez, taking Mary's hand.

She soon forgot her troubles in the pleasures of the *boulanger*. Ramirez's skill on the floor came as no surprise, but her own enjoyment in the long-denied amusement was an unexpected thrill. Mary had been sure she would feel awkward tonight, for she hadn't danced in years, but to her joy the art came back to her with the first strains of music.

Her only uncomfortable moment occurred when it came her time to turn with St. Charles, who was partnering Annabella in the same set. The large young man muttered some compliment, then stared boldly at Mary's décolletage; or was it only her imagination? He said nothing further, but as the dance separated them he looked as thoughtful as Mary had ever seen him.

When next the steps brought them together, St. Charles said, with a keen look at Mary, "My Lady, didn't you forget to put something on tonight?"

Mary drew in her breath. "Sir, I grant you this gown is low, but I assure you—" And then the demands of the other dancers separated them again, leaving her to wonder why St. Charles should have such a puritanical streak. She began to fret, wishing she had brought along a shawl.

When the tune ended Ramirez took Mary's hand again and led her off the floor. "Shall we go out into the conservatory?" he suggested, smiling warmly. "There is something I must say."

Inexplicably, she felt shy. "But perhaps I should return to my aunt . . ."

"My dear, you forget we're married. It won't be scandalous for us to disappear together."

"You're right. I did forget," said Mary with the lightest laugh she could manage. She might indeed be married to this man, but he was still dangerous. Her young girl's reflex—get back to the duenna!—had operated naturally.

She let him take her out of the ballroom through a set of French doors which opened onto a fairyland of potted orange trees, vines, and flower-decked trellises under a fantastic glass roof which arched up like a Gothic cathedral. A few stars and the full moon could be glimpsed in the winter sky, but other lights were few and far between. Many couples had chosen this dim green respite from the ballroom, and Mary and Ramirez had to stroll about for quite a while before they came upon an empty bench.

"Alone at last," said Ramirez with a laugh as they sank down together on the cool stone. "I wanted a private moment to tell you how lovely you look, my dear. Do you suppose that, just for tonight, you could believe me?"

Mary stared at him. "What on earth do you mean, sir?"

He touched her hair. "I mean, my dear Mary, that when it comes to gallantries I seem to be more successful with your cousin, without even meaning to be, than I am with you. Flirting comes naturally to some of us, my dear, and those of you who don't subscribe to the empty game put us at a distinct disadvantage when it comes time to win your love."

To win her love! "Perhaps—" Mary hesitated, not really knowing how to answer him, but feeling she must try "—I need more tangible proofs than a well-turned compliment, sir. I'm no good at flirting; I admit that freely. I have no idea how to flirt back."

She had barely voiced these words when she felt his arm tighten round her waist. "How promising, my dear. Does this mean you wish to flirt back, as you call it? Let me assist you." He looked down at her with that caressing expression she was coming to know well, bent his head to hers, and kissed her.

Mary's first instinct was to freeze; then, the first alarms over, she shocked herself even more than Ramirez had by returning the kisses with all her energy. She knew that she was in imminent danger of losing control of herself for the first time in her life. Strangely, she didn't care, she who had prided herself on being in command of her emotions, if not her life. When Ramirez drew away, after a very long time, Mary reached out and kissed *him*.

"Antonio," she murmured, enraptured.

Gently he detached her, whispering in her ear. "Shh! I've just heard something intriguing."

Mary, gravely insulted at his rejection of her kiss, raised hurt and wondering eyes. He placed his finger on her lips and jerked his head to indicate that what he was interested in was going on behind him.

Curious, Mary peeked through a screen of leaves. She must indeed have been lost in Antonio's company not to have noticed that Annabella was standing not five feet from their hiding place. Beside her was Mr. St. Charles.

The two were obviously engaged in dalliance, for Annabella was speaking in that soft, caressing tone she often used with "Cousin Tony." St. Charles's blond head bent close to Annabella's red-gold curls. They exchanged a lingering kiss. The young man's hand wandered to the front of Annabella's gown. Mary drew in her breath in amazement.

Her next reaction was to get away. Annabella shouldn't be in private with a gentleman, and she certainly shouldn't be letting that gentleman maul her about, but it was still her business and not Mary's.

She made a move to turn away, but Ramirez held her fast. "They were talking," he said into her ear. "Perhaps they'll talk again."

Mary frowned at him and shook her head.

Then Annabella's voice became clear. "Oh, you terrible man," she giggled, detaching the beefy hand from her bosom. "We must stick to the business at hand. What a shame you should be done out of your inheritance, and by her! I knew the moment she came to live with us that there was something strange about her, not even English. I've been trying to get it for you for weeks, you know, ever since you asked me the first time, and now—"

"My love, I knew I could count on you." St. Charles's words were barely audible as his lips laid siege to Annabella's white neck. Obviously speech was over for the moment.

Ramirez gave Mary a look, took her by the hand, and hurried her out of the conservatory. Instead of returning to the ballroom, they left by a side door and went down a corridor. Finally Ramirez stopped at the doorway to a room empty of ballgoers, a small sitting room lit by one lamp. He urged Mary inside and shut the door.

"Your cousin," he said, leading Mary to a sofa and dropping down beside her, "is playing a deep game."

Mary was almost crosser at Annabella for interrupting her own romantic scene than she was curious about what the girl had been saying. One moment she had been coming to some sort of understanding with her husband, the next she was thrust into the position of a Peeping Tom. "She was talking about me, that much was clear. How has she taken it into her head that I've done St. Charles out of an inheritance?"

"I have an idea," said Antonio. His voice was wary. "What do you suppose the object was that she's been trying to get?"

Mary thought for only a second, and then her fingers instinctively touched her bare throat. It was now clear why St. Charles had made that remark during the *boulanger* about her having forgotten to "put something on." He knew of her necklace, and had expected her to wear it.

"I think the same. She is after your necklace," said Antonio.

His words jolted Mary back to the present. She looked at him sharply. "And what is *your* interest in my necklace, sir?"

He didn't give her a direct answer. "The garnet necklace is not just a necklace, isn't that so?"

Guard the garnets as you would your virtue, Doña Inez had told her daughter. She had also said that someone would come forward, when the time was right, to tell Mary the necklace's secret.

Mary looked at her husband with new eyes. He was Spanish; his family had known her mother; was he the one who would make clear to her the secrets she had wondered about for so long? "What *do* you know?" she asked in a softer tone.

He smiled tenderly, regretfully. "I can only tell you for now, my dear, that there is much at stake here. Your ignorance is for your protection. But you must continue to keep that necklace safe."

Mary's consternation showed on her face. "I must have this information, sir. The necklace is my property, brought from the Peninsula. How does Mr. St. Charles even know about it? And you certainly don't mean to tell me that Annabella and her beau have anything to do with—with secrets that might have concerned my mother." Mary could well imagine Annabella wanting the necklace for her own selfish vanity; she could even picture her cousin trying to steal it for St. Charles, if he had somehow cozened her into believing it his "inheritance." But she could not feature Annabella's zeal for the necklace proceeding from any other than personal reasons.

Antonio's expression was grim. "There is much about St. Charles that makes no sense," he said. "I intend to watch him, to see that he does nothing suddenly. You didn't wear the necklace tonight, my love, though it would have looked perfect with your gown. You haven't lost it, have you? It's still safe?"

"Certainly it is. I decided not to wear it because I've been feeling insecure about it. Annabella has been asking to wear it, and I didn't wish to anger her by flaunting it round my neck. There are few things as unpleasant as Annabella in one of her snits."

"I comprehend. When you get home, Mary, you must make certain that the necklace remains secure.

Hide it in a new place. I won't say bring it to me, for you shouldn't even trust me in this particular. Do you understand?''

"No," said Mary slowly, "but I'll do as you say." She was certain of one thing: if Annabella were really after the necklace, the girl would not find it easily.

"There is one more thing I must ask of you. Will you watch your cousin carefully? Without giving away that we suspect her of any wrongdoing?"

Mary's chin lifted in determination. This was a welcome commission. "I certainly will. Her designs on my property aside, she needs a lecture, and I mean to see that she has it this very evening. She shouldn't be so free with her favours. Lady Winter would be horrified.'' She rose from the Egyptian-style sofa, anxious to be about this new duty. Ramirez rose with her.

Suddenly Mary remembered that they were alone in a dimly lit room, and that before seeing St. Charles and Annabella she and Antonio had been engaged in an intimate discussion of their own.

"And you," he said, putting an arm about her shoulders, "do you judge your own behaviour a little less harshly than your cousin's? If your husband should kiss you, even fondle you, would Lady Winter—or you—be horrified?" He pulled her closer and kissed her with great tenderness.

"Don't," said Mary. She looked into his eyes and was surprised by their hurt expression. Though she was at a loss as to why she must not let him continue, she did know there was a reason.

Ramirez seemed to understand better than she did. "I'm going too quickly, am I not?" he suggested, smoothing back a lock of her hair which he had disarranged. "I didn't mean to frighten you."

"Oh, I wasn't frightened," said Mary. His knowing smile in response to those words nearly undid her, and she tried to explain. "We were talking of something else, and then so suddenly we were—well, perhaps I was a bit frightened."

Antonio kissed her cheek quite chastely. "I promised never to force my attentions on you. You need more time, do you not? That is natural. Your father is still against me, and now you find out I've been hiding my knowledge of your necklace. In your place I would be as prudent, my dear."

How well he understood her! Mary was on the point of telling him that she had no plans to be prudent, tonight or any other night, that she would much rather he kissed her again, but something held her back. She did need more time.

"Now," said Antonio, lifting her hand to brush her glove with his lips, "shall we go back to the party? I'll keep a watch on St. Charles, and you may have the delightful task of talking to your cousin."

"Do you think she has the necklace now, and will give it to him?"

"It didn't sound that way, but we must make certain."

Mary was content to return to the ballroom. It being settled that she and Antonio would not get into deeper romantic waters this evening, she felt it to be her duty to speak to Annabella.

She caught up with her cousin in the ladies' retiring room, where Annabella was seated before the dressing table mirror. When she saw Mary she hastily returned an object to her reticule which Mary identified as a hare's foot.

"Cousin, I'm well aware that you rouge, and you needn't hide your equipment from me. I need to speak with you," said Mary.

"I've never rouged in my life. And what could *we* have to talk about?" Annabella's light laugh rang out. "Let's speak in the ballroom, for I've promised every dance and the gentlemen will be wondering where I am." She rose from the dressing table, bestowing a last loving look upon her reflection, and sailed out of the room. Mary had to rush to keep up with her.

She caught at Annabella's spangled sleeve. "I must tell you, Cousin, that your secret is out."

Her cousin stopped in her tracks and looked at Mary in horror. A couple of dowagers brushed past them on their way to the ladies' room, and Annabella instinctively stepped to the wall. Mary followed.

"What the devil do you mean?" asked Annabella. Her voice was belligerent, her expression guilty; but Mary felt she might be reading guilt where it did not exist, because of what she had overheard Annabella say to St. Charles.

"I saw you with St. Charles, Cousin," she said, fighting back the urge to demand of Annabella what she meant by plotting to give her young man the garnet necklace. "In the conservatory. You seemed to be getting along quite well."

"Oh!" Annabella's expression cleared. "Is that all? Well, Mary, I did tell him not to lay hands on me where anyone might observe us, but he is so impetuous! You wouldn't know, my dear, how very insistent a gentleman can be when he wants a small liberty or two. If it will save me in your prudish eyes, though, I'll tell you a little secret: St. Charles and I are engaged."

"You are?" Mary was shocked. "Does your mother know?"

"Oh, no, Mary, and you mustn't tell her. Dear St. Charles is so terribly frightened of Mama, and he doesn't want to let anything out about our attachment until Mama and Papa are more intimately acquainted with his family."

"Oh." Mary frowned, put off by the genuine note of excitement in Annabella's voice. Was her cousin really betrothed, and to a gentleman who was involving her in dishonest schemes?

"I do have your promise, do I not?" Annabella said with her sweetest smile. "You mustn't tell Mama."

Mary nodded; she couldn't feature bringing up such a subject with Lady Winter. "You will promise me in return, Annabella, not to be alone with him anymore? You could be ruined before you know it."

"My heavens, what a prude you are! But there is little enough chance for St. Charles and me to be alone. It's safe to promise." Annabella laughed and swept away without another word. Mary could see a clutch of young men pounce on her cousin when she arrived at the ballroom door and knew that Annabella was safely out of mischief for the evening.

Mary followed and set out for Lady Winter's side, where she expected to stay except when Antonio was dancing with her. Not many young men would risk an interlude with such a scandalous woman as herself, but this made no difference. There was not another man in the room she wished as a partner other than Antonio. She hoped that St. Charles would not claim his set. After hearing her husband's suspicions of the young man, she didn't know if she could manage to be ordinarily civil.

When she passed an open side chamber where refreshments were being served, she glimpsed Antonio talking with St. Charles. The large young man was imbibing freely; a half dozen champagne glasses stood on the table directly in front of him.

Mary had to smile. So that was Antonio's plan to see that St. Charles got into no mischief. She caught her husband's eye for the merest instant. He winked at her.

Moving easily, confidently among the ballgoers, Mary came to rest in a chair beside her aunt's and spent the remainder of the evening thinking of Antonio. Were she and her husband on the brink of a real marriage? The thought terrified her.

Somehow, though, she could not think of the possibility with anything other than a dreamy smile.

CHAPTER ELEVEN

AFTER THE BALL, Mary sat by her bedroom fire, enjoying the shadowy stillness of the room as she mulled over the events of the evening. Memories of everything from Antonio's kisses to suspicions about Annabella and St. Charles were dancing through her mind. The firelight played over the tapestries on the walls, the rich brocade of the chairs and bed covering, and Mary's ball gown, which she couldn't yet bear to remove. She had taken off her shoes and stockings, though, and was waving her toes about in delicious freedom. Her most unladylike trait was a hatred of shoes and boots of all kinds. Doña Inez used to joke that Mary really ought to marry a West Indian so that she might spend her life walking about in the warm sand. Mary smiled at this memory of her mother.

It was only a short step to thoughts of the garnet necklace. Before she took off her pretty gown Mary had a fancy to see herself once more in the necklace; then she would hide it in a new place, as she had promised Antonio. She got up from her fireside seat and crossed the room to the wardrobe, extracted a riding boot, and turned it upside down upon the bed.

Nothing came out. With a shake of her head, Mary took out the other boot from the wardrobe and put her hand inside it. Nothing.

Hesitating for only a moment, she hurried to the inner door which connected the Queen's Bedchamber with the sitting room. It was only a step across the darkened room to the inner chamber where Antonio slept. The shadows of the animal heads on the walls of the sitting room, made lurid and misshapen in the rushlight, looked absolutely menacing as Mary passed them.

In her distress she forgot to knock and simply opened the door. "Antonio!" she cried. "Look at this."

Her husband was in bed, a candle still burned on his night table and he was reading a book. To Mary's surprise, a pair of spectacles were perched upon his nose, giving him a scholarly, strange look quite unlike her private image of him. His chest was bare.

"You aren't dressed," she found herself whispering, inanely, as she stared at the muscled breadth of exposed skin.

"Forgive me the informality; I am in my bed," he answered with an amused look from under ironic dark brows. He removed the spectacles and put them to one side. "My dear, why are you waving your boot in my face?"

"It's my necklace," said Mary, recalled to the present. "I hid it in my riding boot this evening. It's gone."

Ramirez drew in his breath. "Mary, are you certain, absolutely certain?" He moved to get out of bed; Mary instinctively turned her back.

He noted her reaction and stayed where he was. "If you could pass me that dressing gown draped over the chair? Thank you. Don't fear, I won't shock your maidenly sensibilities—yet."

"What are we to do now?" asked Mary. That warmly whispered "yet" had made her cheeks burn, and she tossed him the dressing gown rather than cross the small room to hand it to him. Her eyes remained averted even when he wrapped the silk robe securely round himself and got out of bed.

He was beside her instantly, putting an arm about her. "How did this happen, my darling? When did you last see the necklace?"

"Before the ball I tried it on, then hid it," said Mary. "And I'm sure Annabella didn't come upstairs again after I was down. And we all went to our bedrooms together after the ball. How could she have taken it?"

"Think." Ramirez led her across the small dressing room to his alcove bed; they sat down.

"She must have an accomplice among the servants," Mary said. "Jenny, I would wager." She recalled how the maid had appeared at the door of the Queen's Bedchamber earlier that evening with some trumped-up excuse about sweeping up a spill. Doubtless the girl had watched Mary out of the house, then searched her room.

"The rabbity little chambermaid with the look of a forelock-tugging peasant?"

"That's Jenny to the life. Though I shouldn't accuse the poor girl, for Annabella might be bribing any or all of the servants. I don't understand, Antonio. If Annabella had the necklace, why didn't she simply give it to St. Charles tonight at the ball?"

He shrugged. "There could be any number of reasons. When we heard them talking she obviously didn't have it with her. I would wager she did give it to St. Charles this evening. When she said, in the conservatory, that she would get it for him, she might only have meant that she had hidden it in the cloakroom or some such."

"But I kept an eye on her for the rest of the evening," said Mary. "And you watched St. Charles."

"There was that small space of time while we were talking in the private chamber, after leaving them in the conservatory. They might have managed the exchange then. Well, my dear, it makes no matter. As it turns out, St. Charles won't be making any move to leave the neighbourhood this evening, even if he's stolen a thousand necklaces. I saw that he was drunk as a lord and even helped another gentleman carry him to his bedchamber. He won't move before morning."

"How clever of you." Mary smiled in relief. "And in the morning, Antonio? Will you go to him and demand he give my property back?"

"I assure you I'll do that very thing," said Antonio. "As soon as the sun rises. It is the morning of the hunt, but I expect St. Charles will start for London once he awakens. I'll see he doesn't get there."

"London? Why should he go to London?"

Antonio looked mysterious. "I have an idea that he will," was all he would say. "For tonight, my dear, don't worry. Get some sleep. Tomorrow will be busy." He hesitated and drew Mary closer. "Unless, of course, you would care to—no, pay no attention to me, dear Mary, this small bed would never do for a wedding night." He grinned mischievously. "I cannot let you take advantage of me when we've agreed that we need more time."

Mary was so embarrassed that she said good-night to him in a rush and escaped back to the Queen's Bedchamber, still clutching her riding boot. She was relieved that he hadn't insisted on claiming his conjugal rights at once, but she was also disappointed. Was he not certain that he wanted her? Was that why he had given in so easily to her demand for more time?

She changed into her nightrail, but she didn't sleep. So many thoughts were chasing themselves round her brain that despite repeated efforts to count sheep or concentrate on a book she found herself still pacing the floor and worrying when dawn broke. Her necklace: how strange that the garnets were no longer in her possession; she had so carefully guarded them for three years. Well, Antonio would see to it that she had them back before long.

Wrapping her woolen shawl more closely about herself, Mary paused in her nervous perambulations to open the heavy draperies and let in the light that was trying to edge its way past the cloth. Morning already! She was bound to have a dreadful day, dragging about with heavy-lidded eyes. And she wished most particularly to be alert, to see that Annabella got

up to no mischief. Mary sighed as she parted the curtains and looked out upon the winter landscape. From
this window there was a view of the walled flower
garden beside the expanse of lawn which fronted the
Hall.

What she saw made her eyes open wide. Annabella
was passing through the garden door. Mary could
barely make out the figure in the half-light, but she
was certain that it was Annabella. The girl was wearing a riding habit, easily identifiable by its sweeping
train, and an elaborate hat, a wide-brimmed creation
with a couple of large plumes which Mary privately
considered ridiculously impractical for the serious
business of riding.

She thought quickly. If Annabella had managed to
get herself from her bed not five hours after a ball and
was going out on a ride, it could only be for one reason: to meet St. Charles.

The girl would have to rouse the stables, for she
knew nothing of saddling horses. That would take
some time.

Relieved to be doing something at last, Mary hurried into her own riding dress. She would doubtless
catch up with Annabella before the girl set out, and
Mary had every confidence that she could deal with
her cousin without help.

The household would be stirring before long, for
this was the morning of the hunt and Lady Winter, not
to mention Lord Burnham, liked to set out bright and
early. As for Antonio...he must be told what was
happening. Mary took a deep breath and opened the
connecting door to the next room. This time she only

tapped on the inner door to his private sanctum, for she was terribly afraid he might spring up from his bed if startled from sleep.

She heard a muffled sound. "Antonio!" she called softly.

The door opened. Antonio, his hair rumpled up and his dressing gown wrapped about him, was smiling at her sleepily. "Mary! Did you wish me to join you for a morning ride, my dear? It must be your English blood that gives you such energy the morning after a ball."

"Antonio, Annabella is heading for the stables, and I am going after her," said Mary, deciding on the spot that simple words were warranted. "I suspect she is off to meet St. Charles."

"Say no more, my dear." Instantly alert, Antonio looked grim and determined. "I had actually forgotten for the moment. I doubt that young man will keep any early morning appointments in his jug-bitten condition, but on the off chance . . . you must not go alone. Will you not wait? I'll be ready in an instant."

"No, if I can stop Annabella before she goes on her ride, it will be much the best thing," said Mary. "She must have the necklace still, and I will simply get it back, woman to woman."

"I won't be far behind, my valiant lady," said Antonio, closing the door with a smile.

Mary shook off the feeling that she would be much better off with Antonio's support and went on her way downstairs, quietly taking the side door which she knew was habitually left unbarred for Lady Winter's early-morning convenience. She hurried through the wisps of mist that permeated the garden.

At the stables she found a sleepy-looking boy slouching about the yard. "Have you seen Miss Annabella this morning, Sam?"

"Yes'm, left a moment ago, she did, and wouldn't wait for a groom. Was you to meet her?"

"Yes, that's it. We were to be together. I'm a bit late." Mary was glad the lad had suggested a reasonable story, for she couldn't take a groom on this errand, and Lady Winter was strict about fastening an attendant to either Mary or Annabella when they rode any distance by themselves. "If I could trouble you to saddle Mab?"

"Yes, milady." The boy ran to do her bidding, and Mary nervously strolled about the yard until the dancing grey was led to the mounting block.

Once mounted, Mary was faced with the problem of finding Annabella. She considered the village churchyard to be the most likely spot, since Annabella and St. Charles had met there before, and started for the village, cantering her mount a little way down several side lanes in case Annabella should have chosen one of them for her meeting place.

Mary entered the silent hamlet just as the most industrious cottagers were beginning to go out upon their errands of the day. The few people she saw looked curiously at her, and one helpful old woman reminded Madam that the hunt was in the other direction. Mary nodded and smiled, keeping her eyes peeled for Annabella.

Her vigilance was finally rewarded. In the field beyond the churchyard she thought she saw the edge of
Annabella's riding habit disappearing into a glade of
winter-deadened trees. She urged Mab on; there was
a path skirting the churchyard and connecting with the
field, a right-of-way to the next village.

In a copse of winter beeches Mary came upon the
two she had been expecting to see. Somehow, it was
still a surprise that Annabella and St. Charles really
had chosen to meet, quite as she had guessed. Mary
passed quickly from pride in her own powers of divi-
nation to uneasiness: what could she tell them she was
doing here? She could hardly admit the true reason.

Annabella and her swain were both mounted, and
their faces were incredulous as Mary approached and
brought Mab to a halt beside them. St. Charles, she
noted, looked extremely the worse for wear. His eyes
were puffy and bloodshot, and he wore his clothes, not
with the assurance which usually distinguished him,
but as though they had been tossed on by a pitchfork.

"Mary!" cried Annabella. "What the devil?"

"Such language, Cousin," said Mary as smoothly
as she could. "You need a chaperone, you know, and
here I am—better late than never. I happened to see
you leaving the house and felt you might be planning
something unwise despite our talk last evening." She
turned to St. Charles. "I'm certain you wouldn't wish
to involve Annabella in a scandal, sir."

He was gaping at her as at an apparition. "My lady,
Miss Winter isn't—I mean all respect to Miss Winter."

"Sir, I'm certain you do," replied Mary. She was feeling more easy all the time; she had thought up a plausible reason to seek out the couple, and Antonio would soon catch her up. She need only delay them until he arrived; then he would demand the return of the necklace. "But while your engagement remains private, the proprieties must be adhered to. There is already one scandal in the Winter household, and I'm afraid I caused it. Annabella must be especially careful to raise no eyebrows."

"Engagement?" St. Charles's brow furrowed.

"Yes," said Annabella quickly, "our engagement, St. Charles. I confided in Mary when she saw us in the conservatory."

"Oh." The young man's frown deepened, but he made no protest.

Mary was certain that the engagement had been hatched in her cousin's brain the night before. Annabella was really up to anything.

The conversation foundered. "Well, Mary?" snapped Annabella after some moments of uneasy silence. "Are you really determined to stand over us like—like a duenna? You're being very foolish. This isn't Spain."

"Foolish or not, I consider it my duty," Mary said with a virtuous air, glancing about for Antonio. He was not yet in sight, and she only hoped he would be able to guess the route she and these miscreants had taken.

"We had as well go home, then," said Annabella. "St. Charles is going to the hunt, aren't you, sir? He mustn't be late for Lord Burnham."

"That's true," said the young man. He tipped his hat to the ladies. "Can't disappoint his lordship. He's counting on me; whole point of the visit, isn't it?"

"Is it?" said Mary with a significant look. According to Ramirez, once St. Charles had the stolen garnet necklace he would go to London with it. She doubted he was really planning to attend the hunt.

But he was rattling on at a great rate about Lord Burnham's special need of him, and Mary began to think Antonio must be wrong in this particular. Such a zealous sportsman would certainly not miss the hunt. Even if he had the necklace with him, he would think it safe enough to partake of the pleasures of the chase before going about his thieving business.

"Good day, ladies," said St. Charles abruptly, at the end of his recital, and he urged his roan hunter into action.

Unfortunately the roan was close to Strawberry and made that placid horse shy by kicking close to the beast's head. Annabella jerked on the reins as St. Charles disappeared from view; Strawberry made a halfhearted flail of her forelegs into the air; and before Mary could blink, her cousin was slipping from the saddle, screeching.

"Ooh!" said Annabella angrily from her new position on the ground. "I'm dreadfully in pain. Mary?"

"I can hardly lift you up again," said Mary, stifling a giggle. "You aren't really hurt, are you?"

"Much you care," grumbled Annabella. She didn't rise from the ground, merely picked a twig off her skirt and waited.

Mary shrugged, dismounted a touch more gracefully than Annabella, and assisted the other girl to her feet. "Oh, dear, you've a dreadful stain on the back of your habit."

"Oh!" Annabella burst into angry tears. Obviously she was overtired and overwrought.

The sound of hoofbeats made itself heard over Annabella's sniffles, and Mary looked up to see Antonio, mounted on his black Amadís, arriving at last. He swung down from his horse.

"Well?" He spoke in a harsh voice to Annabella. "Where is the necklace?"

Mary's eyes opened wide on hearing him address Annabella in such a blunt way. So did Annabella's.

"How dare you?" Annabella gasped. "I've just fallen from my horse, Cousin Tony."

"I am sorry to hear that, ma'am. Where is my wife's garnet necklace?"

Annabella should have been sly enough to deny all knowledge of the bauble; perhaps it was her distraught state that made her laugh harshly and say, "It's too late. That thief—" and she indicated a surprised Mary "—has been foiled at last. I gave the necklace to St. Charles only a moment ago, before she arrived to spy on us. Now he has his inheritance back, thanks to me."

Mary stared.

Antonio was more active. Grasping Annabella by the shoulders, he snarled, "You foolish creature! Don't you know that what you've done makes you a traitor to your country?"

Annabella and Mary both looked at him in amazement. Never had Mary seen him so angry. He let Annabella go with a wrenching movement and remounted his horse. "Where did he go?"

"He spoke of going to the hunt," said Mary. "But you remember that you thought he would be off to London once he had the necklace."

"No matter. Hilltop House is on the London road. I won't waste much time, regardless." Antonio smiled down at Mary. "Take care, my dear. I'll have your necklace back in your hands before you know it." He turned to Annabella. "And you. You had better pray, dear Cousin, that no one finds out your role in this." He rode off before Annabella could even snap at him.

"He won't get the necklace back," said Annabella with a toss of her head, glaring at Mary. "St. Charles can take care of himself."

"You'd better hope he can," said Mary darkly, wondering what Antonio could have meant by saying Annabella was a traitor to her country.

She watched her husband ride away. Then, when he was out of sight, she turned an angry face on Annabella. "And now, my dear Cousin, perhaps you'd be good enough to tell me how you stole the necklace out of my room?"

"*I*, stoop to such a thing as stealing?" Annabella laughed. "I had Jenny do it."

"That silly maid! I knew it."

Annabella's expression was mischievous, her tone confiding, as she said, "She searched your room after we'd all gone to the ball. I had to change the plans rather suddenly, you know. We had thought all along that you would wear the garnets to the ball, and then St. Charles would have got the necklace from you by some sort of sleight of hand. I believe he planned to pretend to make love to you. When I saw you weren't wearing it, though, I thought it was much the better idea simply to have Jenny go to your room and take it while we were out.''

''How matter-of-factly you speak of stealing some-one else's property,'' said Mary in a wondering tone.

''Stealing? St. Charles has told me all about you, Mary. You needn't play the innocent with me. I know you're the thief among us.''

''Oh, that's right. He told you some wild story, and naturally you believed him.'' Mary paused and looked her cousin in the eye. ''Now, what I want to know is how on earth you could be so stupid.''

''You are the one who kept your stolen property in a boot,'' said Annabella with a toss of her head. ''Now I am going to the hunt. I must see that dear St. Charles isn't embarrassed by that horrid foreigner.''

''I thought he was your 'Cousin Tony,''' said Mary sweetly. Turning her back on Annabella, she led Mab over to a fallen log and used it as a mounting block.

''Mary!'' said Annabella imperiously. ''I cannot possibly do that. I will need help to mount.''

''Isn't that too bad?'' Mary hid a smile. She rode away without a backward glance.

HER FIRST INSTINCT was to follow Ramirez in the direction of Hilltop House and London, but she repressed this and sensibly headed for Woodbank Hall, reasoning that she would only be in the way during any confrontation with St. Charles. When she arrived back at the house Shaldon told her that Lady Winter had left for the hunt not long before. Sir Egbert, as was his habit, had decided not to attend despite his wife's protests that he owed that mark of respect to his neighbour.

Mary went to her room to consider further the notion of going to the hunt herself. Surely it would do no harm to be on the spot . . .

On the ornate dressing table of the Queen's Chamber was a clumsily folded note, addressed to Mary. She opened it and read, *"Come to my room at once. Papa."*

Puzzled, Mary confined her toilette to taking off her riding hat and gloves and tossing down her crop; she hurried along to her father's room. It was unusual for him to wake this early in the morning.

To her surprise, Captain Winter was fully dressed and out of bed. Seated in an easy chair in front of the fire, he was positively twitching in impatience.

"There you are! Thought you'd never get here," he said. "They tell me that husband of yours has left the house."

"Why, yes, there's a little problem he had to clear up," responded Mary. "What in heaven's name roused you so early, Papa? Is something wrong? I'm glad to see you dressed, but are you certain you're well enough?"

Captain Winter made no answer to this; he motioned Mary to the chair opposite his own. She sat down.

"Well, Papa?" When the silence had extended for over a minute, Mary became impatient.

Sighing, her father raised his eyes to the portrait of his late wife over the mantel. Mary looked, too. Was it only her imagination, or did Doña Inez's expression seem more accusing than ever? Mary shivered, recalling her little-girl fantasy that the portrait could tell when she had been making mischief.

"Your mother," said the captain, "would have my head for revealing the secret. But the time's come, Mary. The time's come."

Mary simply sat, motioning him to continue.

He cleared his throat. "You know, child, how I barked at you when I was sick? You said that I mentioned your garnets when I was in the fever, and I denied it when I came to myself?"

"I did think that was rather strange," said Mary carefully. She opened her mouth to tell her father the necklace was missing, but something made her change her mind. "What do you know about my necklace, Papa?"

Captain Winter's eyes slid sideways and fixed on the fire. "My dear, there is a secret about the garnets, and you've never known it. Your mother and I thought it best you didn't know. Now I'm aware Inez told you the garnets were special, when she gave 'em to you."

Mary nodded. "She told me that I was to keep the garnets safe, that they were unusual in some way that would be revealed to me in time. You know that."

"And now I'm doing the revealing," said Captain Winter. "You're an heiress, my girl. A great heiress. The necklace—"

"An heiress? You always say we're poor as rats—your very phrase," Mary interrupted.

"It's the necklace. Your mother wanted you to keep it safe because she knew that one day you would have to present it to the banker who is keeping your inheritance. Your treasure."

"My treasure?" Mary's eyes widened.

"Gold and some jewellery, a large casket that was smuggled out of Spain at the start of the trouble," said Captain Winter quickly. He was becoming more excited as he spoke. "The necklace, you see, will be the banker's assurance that you are the true heiress. The treasure can only be given up to the person who presents the necklace."

"An inheritance for me," Mary said in wonder. The idea was almost beyond her power to comprehend. She had never supposed that the garnets' secret was wealth. She had imagined, on the contrary, that the stones might have some political significance. Apparently Doña Inez had been asking Mary to safeguard her own future when she had told her to guard the garnets as she would her virtue.

Strangely, the notion that the garnets' secret was only a financial one was a disappointment of sorts. But many things suddenly became clear: why St. Charles would concoct an elaborate scheme to get the necklace, why Antonio assumed St. Charles would go straight to London once he had the necklace in his possession. "This bank where the treasure was placed is a London bank, of course."

"Bank of England," her father affirmed.

"And Antonio knows about it." Mary's eyes widened. "That's why—Papa, that is why you were so upset when he married me! You knew that he was aware of my inheritance."

The captain shifted uncomfortably in his chair. "I suspected it, no more. His family knew your mother in Spain. I felt he might have come by the knowledge, though it was to be a great secret. Even you weren't to know!"

"But he did know," said Mary, half to herself. "Before we married he must have known. He—it is a lot of money, isn't it, Papa?"

"A great plenty. Enough to ensure our futures, Daughter."

"Enough to marry somebody for?"

Captain Winter merely shrugged.

Mary's mind easily supplied the details that had always been missing from her courtship. Here, at long last, was the missing motive, the real reason Antonio had married her so suddenly, and with such an apparently strong desire for the union. Money! Her heart sank, and her cheeks were flooded with red at the thought of her behaviour with him at the ball, even the intimate fashion in which she had treated him early this morning, running to him because—her necklace was missing! No wonder he was so anxious to get it back.

The sick feeling in the pit of Mary's stomach nearly overwhelmed her, and she glared at her father. "Why didn't you tell me of this at once, sir, on my wedding day? How could you let me go on, day after day, married to that man? Why, I might have—" She stopped speaking abruptly. She had been very close to letting her husband make love to her last night, but how could she say such a thing to Papa?

Captain Winter understood her. "Well, Daughter, you'd said you weren't lettin' him touch you. That set my mind at rest. I spent some time mulling over whether I should tell you this, or whether I should let things stand until I could figure out how to get the marriage set aside. You're of age, worse luck, and consented to it, and according to Egbert's notion of the law it ain't easy to get a marriage annulled."

Mary nodded dismally, thinking over the events of that strange marriage day in London. It was surely impossible that Ramirez had planned any of it in advance, for no one could have predicted Mary breaking away from Annabella and striking out on her own. But the fact that Ramirez had stayed by her after his rescue of her—he had recognized her, beyond a doubt, from Lady Holland's party. He might easily have found out her identity there, have approached to help her with Papa because she had been identified to him as Doña Inez's daughter.

Mary put her hand to her head. A plausible scenario of her marriage was playing out in her mind. First, the party. Lord Holland pointing her out to Ramirez, and Ramirez's likely thoughts: he was poor now, ruined, and here was a girl with a large treasure for a dowry. A little plain, perhaps, but Ramirez would have no difficulty in employing his charm, no matter who the quarry...

"I can't believe this, Papa," she felt bound to say. But the poison was already at work. Her hard-won confidence that such a handsome, worldly young man could care for her, plain Mary Winter, was slipping by the minute. For Ramirez, the imbroglio at Tattersall's had doubtless been a stroke of luck. He hadn't had to go to the trouble of seeking Mary out or courting her: she had fallen into his arms.

"Now, now, m'dear." Captain Winter reached over and patted her hand. Her woebegone face must have aroused his sympathy. "There's more than one fish in the sea. The only question is, do you want this one to have your money?"

"No," said Mary fiercely.

"Good girl. I knew you had a lot of family feeling. Your mother—" Captain Winter gazed up at the portrait again, then looked away "—she'd be pleased. Wouldn't want you to give in to a fortune hunter. Trust me."

Mary also glanced up at the portrait of Doña Inez. To her eye, Mama's expression was more severe than ever. She fumbled for a handkerchief. "Papa, I wish you had told me this earlier."

Her father scowled. "M'dear, perhaps I was wrong to try to protect you as long as possible, but the important thing is, I've come clean at the last. Now we've got to get that treasure out of the bank today, do you hear? Before Ramirez gets wind that I've told you all. We'll put it in some other bank in my name—"

Mary's eyes flashed. "Papa, I'm wondering if Ramirez is the only greedy one in this instance. It would solve everything, would it, if I were simply to put this alleged money in your name?"

"Why, Mary. You know I'd always share with you," muttered Captain Winter.

"Oh, Papa." Mary sighed. "You can't blame me for being confused, and I shall need some time to consider the consequences. But you're right about one thing. If that man has married me counting on this money, he shall not get a penny."

Captain Winter was all cheerfulness at this turn in the conversation. "Today is the best chance we'll have to go to London without interference, with that nosy Letitia at the hunt and this one of Ramirez's days at the fencing rooms. I got Egbert to promise me the loan of the chaise. We must leave at once. Go get the necklace, and we'll be off."

"Well, Papa, you've been confessing things to me," said Mary. She hated to ruin his exuberant mood, but she had no choice. "Now it's my turn. The necklace is missing."

The portrait of Doña Inez seemed almost alive as the magnificent woman's black eyes glared down directly at the viewer. Both Mary and her father glanced at the picture and cringed. For some moments they kept silent.

"Missing?" Captain Winter finally said. "You careless girl, then find it. Now!"

"I didn't lose the necklace, Papa. It was stolen."

The captain's light eyes bulged, and he started forward; then he leaned back in his chair, grumbling. "Too late. That Spaniard has outfoxed me."

"He didn't take it," said Mary. "The necklace disappeared while we were at the ball last night, and Annabella has admitted having a maid steal it so that she could give it to her beau, Mr. St. Charles.''

Captain Winter's eyes nearly popped at this. ''What's that you say? Who are you talking about?''

''The secret of the necklace wasn't well kept, except from me,'' said Mary with a shrug. ''Annabella's beau St. Charles knew of it and lied to Annabella, telling her that the necklace was the property of his family and that I had stolen it. So she arranged to give it back to him. Antonio went after him a little while ago to get the necklace back.'' She sighed. ''He said he'd return it to me, but—''

''You'll grow old waiting for that day,'' her father finished. ''We'd best go to the bank anyway, my child. We can tell our side of the story.''

''You may go to all the banks you like, Papa,'' said Mary. ''I intend to follow Antonio now. Perhaps he's seeking out St. Charles at the hunt, or perhaps he's gone after him to London. I must face him with this. He can't be allowed to get away without answering to me for what he's done.'' Her voice broke, and she turned her head so that her father wouldn't see her tears.

''You take a groom with you!'' shouted her father as she left his room, nearly running in her anxiety to be on her way.

But Mary knew she must face the coming task alone.

CHAPTER TWELVE

SOON THE HUNTER Mab's long, powerful legs were covering the five-mile distance between Woodbank Hall and Hilltop House, Lord Burnham's seat. Mary knew there was a gala hunt breakfast planned for after the chase, but the riders must assemble beforehand, and, the social proclivities of the English county families being what they were, the hunt might not start promptly. Ramirez would likely have plenty of time to confront St. Charles before the pack was let loose—if St. Charles had indeed chosen to attend the hunt.

Mary hoped Ramirez would not have to follow the hunt. Would Aunt Winter, Lord Burnham or anyone else in the riding ever forgive a foreigner engaged in quite a different pursuit for disrupting their sport?

When Mary rode up the drive of the palatial Hilltop House, the quiet of the surroundings gave her pause. There was in the air a suggestion of excitement just past. She felt in her bones that the party was already gone.

The footman at the door informed Mary that she was indeed too late. The riders had gone out a full half hour before. They had expected to find in the south field; the man had heard the house party's conversation, and the famous dog fox of the district had been the main topic of discussion, along with the animal's probable whereabouts. Yes, the footman believed Mr. St. Charles had been with the others. Milady's husband, Lord Ramirez, had called at the house moments after the hunt's departure and had gone after the others.

Thanking the man, Mary remounted and sped in the direction he had indicated. The hunters, the dogs, the spectators who gathered in the fields to see the hunt go by: all must be pleased with this sunny, cold day. Everyone, that is, except the fox.

The south field was empty of everything save some severely trampled grass. Mary hailed two small boys who were playing near a hedge and asked them which way the hunt had taken.

One of the lads was of an age and had enough interest in hunting to be able to contribute much more than a pointing finger. "They found in the bottom of the field, mum, and I think it was the old dog fox, the one what Lord Burnham swears he'll have one day, and old Dolly, that's 'is lordship's prize bitch, she give voice and all the rest of 'em goes streaming after. Down that way, it was."

"Many thanks. I hope you can join the hunt one day," returned Mary, smiling into the child's bright, excited face. Then she urged Mab on southward.

The horse's thrill at the hard ride was contagious. By the time Mary came in sight of the last few stragglers of the hunting party, she was truly exhilarated and would have been enjoying her day in happier circumstances. Despite her vexing mission, she must rejoice as any devoted horsewoman would to feel the crisp air cooling her face and blowing the cobwebs from her mind.

"Have you seen Lord Ramirez or Mr. St. Charles?" she asked of the first lady she reached, a haughty young woman she remembered meeting at the ball.

"My word! I never expected to see *you* here, ma'am," returned the woman, in a tone she might have used to express the sighting of a spider in her soup.

"Oh, I'm not here as a guest," said Mary. She was in too much of a hurry to feel hurt that the nine days' wonder of Tattersall's had gone into its fourth week. "I have a message to convey. Have you seen the gentlemen?"

Either the lady had not, or she thought it best not to direct Mary further into the hunting field. She merely shrugged in answer. Mary had no choice but to keep riding.

The few people she dared to question after this hadn't seen either man, but someone mentioned that the master was up ahead and that the fox would surely be cornered soon.

Mary could hear the baying of the dogs as she directed Mab through a small birch copse and out again into another brown field. And then she saw a fine sight: the pack of dogs, flying down a hillside in the distance, Lord Burnham in his hunting pink charging after, and several other riders behind him. Was that Lady Winter, the female in the scarlet habit? Mary would wager it was. Then she looked again at the large male rider directly on the heels of the master. They were too far away for Mary to make out features, but surely that was St. Charles, the stocky figure, the sturdy roan horse . . .

Then another rider appeared from a wooded area to the side. Ramirez! His black stallion Amadís was perfectly recognizable, if he himself was not at this distance. Mary watched as her husband came even with St. Charles and probably shouted at him over the swarm of dogs which now surrounded them.

She looked again. At the bottom of the hill a tangle of dogs, the exultant cries of Lord Burnham, the blasting of a horn, all announced that the poor dog fox—or whichever fox it was—had run out of luck.

She had been on the point of urging Mab down the hill, but this put a different complexion on matters. Mary didn't care to be in on the kill now, any more than she had in her childhood, when she had got sick after being taken to her first and only bullfight. Ramirez could just as well be confronted once he was out of the thick of things.

From her vantage point she saw St. Charles break from the twisting mass of dogs and riders and go off, springing his horse. He jumped a hedge. Ramirez was off after him, sailing Amadís over the hawthorn in an effortless manner. The two riders were soon no more than specks on the horizon. Mary decided to skirt the scene of the kill and follow.

Her horse Mab gloried in the chance of jump the hedge, though the animal did grow skittish at the sight of the swirling mass of hounds, horses, and shouting men round which Mary directed her. Mary kept her seat easily despite the fact that she hadn't had the chance to jump a hedge in some time. Giving Mab her head, she sped after the two men—or she hoped she did. They were now out of sight.

She hadn't ridden for ten minutes before she came upon another scene of carnage: Ramirez and St. Charles, dismounted, exchanging blows in the dirt of a barren field while their heaving horses waited patiently.

Fascinated, she watched. St. Charles, for all his superior girth, seemed to be on the losing end. Mary wasn't surprised; she remembered how Ramirez had trounced Tom Trumble, a man twice his size.

Just as Ramirez applied a jarring blow to St. Charles's jaw and the larger man staggered backward, a flash of red darted by Mary. She blinked, watching the small streak of fur leap over a wide stream with the aid of an overhanging branch and disappear into the wood beyond. A fox.

She had no more than identified the beast when a pack of exuberant dogs swarmed past her and clustered at the stream, yelping and baying. Some of the hounds pattered out into the water, but the rushing current was too strong to tempt them further.

Next Lord Burnham, followed by Lady Winter and a half dozen other riders, thundered past. Seeing the halt at the stream, the master let out a howl that would have sounded well coming from one of his hounds.

Mary didn't understand. She had been so certain that the dogs had the fox and were in the process of tearing it apart when she'd gone past the hunt earlier, at the bottom of that hill.

The whole business of the hunters' arrival had taken only seconds. Mary returned her attention to the other point of interest: Ramirez and St. Charles. Her eyes widened in fear. In the moment she had been distracted, St. Charles had pulled out a wicked-looking knife.

Antonio was unarmed, but his knowledge of fencing came to his aid as he danced and feinted round his burly opponent, his wiry, muscular form seeming to mock the ungainliness of St. Charles.

Finally St. Charles tired of this, gave a menacing roar and lunged forward, knife thrusting.

Antonio neatly stepped aside, and the other man lost his balance and fell to the ground. Antonio set a foot on St. Charles's chest while he twisted the knife from the man's grasp. Then, holding the weapon at its owner's chin, Antonio calmly went through St. Charles's pockets.

Only when Mary relaxed did she realize how rigid with terror she had been for those few moments. She dismounted and ran to her husband, nearly tripping on St. Charles, who lay passive on the ground, a disgusted expression on his broad face. "I saw it all, or most of it. You are so clever, Antonio."

He smiled. "Mary! I thought you'd be here; I didn't know how, but I felt you'd manage it. I have the honour of returning to you your property." And he opened one hand to reveal the garnet necklace, which he clasped around the high neck of Mary's black riding habit.

Mary remembered now that she was angry with him; her fear for his safety had put her grievances out of her mind. She touched the necklace. Why had he given it back, if he was as despicable a character as she thought him to be?

"Antonio," she said, "I know."

"You know?"

"About the treasure."

"Oh!" The spark of recognition in his eyes made her certain that he knew all about it. "I didn't think you did, somehow."

"My father told me not an hour ago that I've been an heiress all this time. The necklace is the key to a treasure. And it follows that I now know, at last, why you married me," said Mary, managing to speak coolly, impersonally.

"The captain told you that?" His face darkened in anger.

"Yes, he did." Mary returned his angry look with one of absolute fury.

"You think *that* of me?"

His voice was incredulous, and Mary lifted her chin in defiance. "What else am I to think?"

He snapped back, "What you please, evidently. If you would allow me to explain—"

"I don't want your excuses," Mary interrupted. "What I want to know is this: who is St. Charles, Antonio, and how did he know of my necklace?"

"He is someone I've been looking for for a long time." He seemed relieved to change the subject, and Mary, who wanted no falsifications of his avaricious desire to marry her, was quite willing to talk civilly on another subject. "I'm glad the hunt passed this way," he continued. "I must send one of these gentlemen for a magistrate. This man, Mary," and he pointed to the silent St. Charles, still scowling from his position on the ground, "is a French spy. He has been seeking to divert the treasure to the Bonapartists. That's why he came to the neighbourhood."

"And that's why he courted Annabella," said Mary in instant understanding. She and her cousin had both been made use of in this affair of the necklace. "How did he come by the information?"

"The affairs of France and the affairs of Spain are closely entwined," said Ramirez with a shrug. "Though not as closely as the French would like them to be. They have their agents everywhere, and I don't doubt they had one in Spain at the time the treasure was gathered."

Gathered! That was a strange term. "Only fancy such an English-looking young man a French spy," said Mary, shaking her head.

"What have we here?" a familiar voice put in, and Mary turned to see Aunt Winter approaching them, plodding through the fresh dirt with no regard for her costume. "Mary, child. It ain't good form to pass the master, you know. Say! I thought you knew better than to wear jewels with a—oh! That's your neck-lace. Much better, my dear, had you worn it last night."

"Aunt, I'm wearing it because..." Mary hesitated, wondering how best to impart the strange and complex tale of the necklace to someone who hadn't heard anything about it. She decided there was no easy way. "What about the fox?" she asked, to get her aunt's mind on to other things.

Lady Winter snorted in disgust. "The blasted pack was thrown off the scent by a *dead* fox in the field back there, likely planted by some one of Lord Burnham's tenants, for he's not a popular man among the yeomanry. But that's neither here nor there. Meanwhile our old enemy, the dog fox, came on. Finally old Dolly picked up the scent again. There's no dog like her, up to every rig, she ain't fooled for long. Then we find the trail ends at the water. Burnham's fit to tear apart the first thing he sees."

Mary said, "The fox sprang over the stream by that hanging branch. I'm sorry, Aunt." She did rejoice for the old dog fox, safe for another day, but she had the courtesy to do so privately.

"Now, what's this? Mr. St. Charles has been taken sick? We must send for the apothecary." Aunt Winter gave one last sigh over the fox and returned her attention to the project at hand.

"No, Lady Winter, actually the gentleman is my prisoner," said Ramirez, with a bow. "He had my lady's garnet necklace, and I got it back. Before he could sell the secrets it holds to the French. I have every reason to believe he's working for the Bonapartists."

"What! This gentleman? But I'd practically settled on him for my Annabella. Did you see him ride this morning? She couldn't want a better man."

"Unfortunately," said Ramirez stiffly, "he is also a traitor who sought to turn over a large Spanish fortune to the French cause. He would see this country invaded as soon as ride over it."

"Mary, child! Can this be true?" demanded Aunt Winter.

"I think so, Aunt," said Mary. "Mr. St. Charles has been acting quite suspiciously, and I think he's been using Annabella to get at the necklace. It's complicated."

"Someone's been using Annabella for selfish ends, you say?" Aunt Winter suddenly looked more cheerful. "Using Annabella, not the other way about? Well!"

At this point a disgusted groan from St. Charles brought his still undignified position to their attention. Ramirez aided him to sit up. By the time St. Charles got himself into a more comfortable situation, several of the disappointed huntsmen had wandered over to see what the altercation was about. Only Lord Burnham remained at the stream, cursing his fate and the victorious dog fox.

"Good Lord," moaned Mr. St. Charles, seeing the crowd, and he shut his eyes. Then, in apparent resignation, he opened them again.

"Mr. St. Charles," said Lady Winter, pushing forward, "my niece will have it that you're a spy and a jewel thief. Is this true?"

St. Charles's face was set and cold as he responded, "My political allegiances may be different from the rest of yours, that is all."

"Ah! I also hear you've no real interest in my Annabella. What do you say to that?"

St. Charles stared at this turn in the conversation. "The young lady is delightful," he answered with a shrug. "Many young ladies are. But she had the added advantage of living in the house with the necklace I had to have. She has made a charming dupe.'' Turning from Lady Winter, he addressed Ramirez in French. His accent was so clear and true that all doubts about him flew from Mary's mind. Those perfect Parisian tones simply could not be the result of a British education.

Ramirez responded in the same language. Mary had forgotten much of the French she had learned as a child, but she gathered that St. Charles was asking what would happen to him now, and Ramirez was responding that the other would be taken into custody and released, should he prove innocent.

St. Charles sighed deeply and swore a Gallic oath.

''A Frenchie!'' exclaimed Lady Winter. ''Fancy that. I'd as soon believe John Bull an opera dancer.''

Excited conversation broke out among the gentlemen, and Ramirez asked one of them to ride for the magistrate. He, Ramirez, would remain with the accused until the authorities could return.

''Er, there won't be any need to ride,'' said one of the men, running a finger around his neckcloth and glancing uncomfortably in the direction of the stream. ''You see, Lord Burnham is the magistrate hereabouts.''

Ramirez burst out laughing.

Mary tried to contain her own nervous hilarity; the picture of Lord Burnham having to arrest his houseguest and newest favourite did have its element of humour.

Suddenly the sound of hoofbeats made the whole party turn. Annabella, her oddly cocked hat and

muddied skirts testimony to a wild ride if not a fall,
tumbled from Strawberry's thick back and rushed to
the scene.

"Oh, dear St. Charles, has that beast hurt you?"
she cried, casting herself down upon the ground to
encircle with her arms a very surprised John St.
Charles. "Don't worry, we'll soon prove he's an evil
thief, just like my cousin."

St. Charles's eye met Lady Winter's, and he
shrugged as he tried to dislodge the girl from his coat-
front.

"I'll never fail you," continued Annabella with a
romantic sigh.

The other members of the hunt raised their eyebrows at this. The buzz of conversation grew more
furtive, and, Mary thought from the snatches she
could hear, less than flattering to cousin Annabella.

"Annabella, dear child," Lady Winter said in a tone
of barely suppressed pleasure, "that's a Frenchie spy
you're flinging yourself at. Best hold off."

Annabella glared at her mother. "Mama, perhaps
this isn't the time to tell you, but Mr. St. Charles and
I are to be married. And you're wrong, you know. He
can't be a spy. He's told me all about himself."

St. Charles groaned at this and gave up trying to
loosen Annabella's tenacious hold round his neck. The
conversation among the gentlemen grew even louder
and more excited in tone.

Mary felt a sharp stab of pity for her cousin. The
girl had as good as ruined herself by claiming an engagement to a French spy. Whether the plans for
marriage had been hatched in Annabella's brain the

day before, or whether St. Charles had sweetened his demands of the girl with such a promise, was beside the point. Annabella's reputation was in shreds.

"Cousin Annabella." Ramirez stepped forward. "You cannot marry that traitor. If I might assist you back to your horse? You had best return home now."

Annabella tossed her head, but she did cast one uncomfortable look at the man she still held captive on the ground. St. Charles turned a colourful brick shade and looked away.

"John! What does this mean?" Annabella cried. "Tell them all the truth! Mary and her husband were out to cheat you of your inheritance. Naturally I had to help you get the necklace back." She bestowed a venomous glare on Mary. "Though I see you have it now, you selfish thing."

Mary shrugged, not knowing what to say. If it had not been useless, she would have appealed to Annabella to be silent before she made herself seem even more guilty of collaboration with a French spy. Heavens, the whole county was standing by as audience!

Ramirez seemed to realize that. Clearing his throat loudly, he said, "My cousin is obviously overwrought. A spasm, I think. She doesn't know what she's saying. Perhaps we could take her home at once, Lady Winter?"

"I'm not going home!" cried Annabella, "And Mr. St. Charles is not French. He's as English as I am, and more English than either one of you!" She stared spitefully at Ramirez and Mary.

No one, including St. Charles, had anything to say to these dramatics. Annabella looked about her at the sea of interested faces. Finally she unclasped her arms from round the burly neck of her erstwhile suitor.

"Ramirez is right, girl. This is no place for you," said Lady Winter, rolling her eyes at Ramirez as she spoke to her daughter. "You're going home. And I, for one, am getting to the bottom of this right now."

"So am I," added Mary. "You others may go home if you wish. I am going into London. To the bank."

"Bank?" A dozen voices registered astonishment at this seeming non sequitur. Ramirez approached Mary and looked full into her eyes.

"You are right," he said. "We must get to the bottom of this for your sake. And at once."

"You shan't go anywhere without me," Lady Winter put in.

"Or me," chimed in Annabella. She had risen to her feet at last, and now she strode over to the others, eyes blazing. "What on earth does a silly bank have to do with any of this?"

There was a pause, and Ramirez seemed to resign himself to the participation of the Winter ladies. He didn't even attempt to dissuade them, which irked Mary a little. She did see, however, that any such effort would be doomed to failure. Annabella and Lady Winter were exactly alike in their determination.

"To London!" said Ramirez. "Ladies, shall we ride?"

CHAPTER THIRTEEN

THE PARTY OF FOUR had not gone beyond the first field before Annabella's shrill complaints about her discomfort drew a sigh from Ramirez.

"It would be best to take Cousin Annabella home and then go on to London. These horses are winded from the hunt in any case."

"You won't take me anywhere and leave me," snapped Annabella. Never had Mary heard her use that tone of voice to a man. "I'm coming along."

Lady Winter said, "We'd best take the carriage if we're stopping by the Hall. Two carriages, if she insists on coming."

"Mama!"

A robust mother-daughter brangle enlivened the rest of the ride to Woodbank Hall. Ramirez and Mary rode side by side, not looking at each other.

They were turning in at the gates when Mary said, "Since we are here, I insist that Papa come along to London." She paused and looked Ramirez in the eye. "Unless you are afraid of what he'll reveal about my inheritance."

Ramirez shrugged. "By all means, let him come if he wants to. And we must make all speed, you know, to arrive before the banks close."

Mary thought she knew her father well enough to vouch for his participation in the scheme. When she burst into his room and poured out a confused story about Annabella's beau being a spy who wanted the necklace, Captain Winter became instantly alert. His watery blue eyes gleamed when he saw the garnets safely clasped around his daughter's neck.

"So Ramirez claims a Frenchie spy took it?" he said with a snort. "I'll wager it was pretty easy for him to get some friend to play the part of a thief, then Ramirez gets the necklace back, makes you grateful, and walks off with your fortune."

"Gracious, Papa! Evidence does suggest that Mr. St. Charles was working for the French. He probably even is half-French. His pure accent, for one thing."

Captain Winter shook his head. "Every Englishman is taught French."

"Precisely. And you know how most of them sound in any foreign language, especially French. Mr. St. Charles spoke like a native of Paris. I could pick up the exact inflections of old Madame Fleur, who taught me."

"And you call that proof?" The captain had been speaking from his bed, where he had retired in the aftermath of his earlier disappointment over the necklace. Now he flung aside the coverlet. He was fully clothed except for coat and boots. "Lucky I got dressed this morning," he added, slightly straightening his rumpled attire.

"We may not trust Ramirez, Papa, but I have the necklace now. He gave it back to me." Mary took the bauble from around her neck and put it safely into the pocket of her habit. "And if he takes the treasure now, as he has every legal right to do, he'll probably leave us and we can be as we were." Though she struggled to speak in a cheerful tone, her heart turned over at this idea.

"Not quite as we were. I can't provide for you," said Captain Winter darkly. "With me on half pay, we'll be stuck at Egbert's forever. I wish we could go back, Mary." He sighed, and she knew that he was thinking of his injuries.

Her father had never been one to care about money one way or the other when he had been able to earn enough for his family's needs in the work that had been his life: the military. A feckless sort, he hadn't even been certain how much his pay was, for Mary could remember her mother marvelling at the impracticality of men. Mary sensed that Papa's obsession with the treasure now was not simple greed; it was only a fixed idea born out of the helpless feeling he had of being unable to take care of himself or his daughter in the future.

Mary didn't think Ramirez would take the money and disappear. Even should he come into legal possession of the whole—whatever sum that might be—he would share it evenly with her and Papa. The law might all be on the husband's side in questions of property, but Mary could feel, deep within her, that Ramirez was too honourable to abscond. *Now that the whole affair is out in the open!* her suspicious mind added.

If she could only know whether he had married her *entirely* because of the inheritance! He had seemed insulted at the idea. But he had admittedly known of this Spanish fortune when he married her. Surely that argued against his honesty.

"Come along, you two!" The voice of Lady Winter rang down the gallery and penetrated the thick door of Papa's room. "The coach is at the door."

"Her, too?" Captain Winter sighed. "It needed only that." Mary helped him into his coat and a pair of pumps, explaining as best she could that not only Lady Winter but Annabella would be their companions on this strange outing. The captain was appalled, but he refused to back out of the trip to London.

Mary found herself wedged between Papa and Ramirez in the coach while Lady Winter and Annabella exchanged verbal punches from the forward seat. "Your exposure as a thief and a spy's accomplice, Annabella, puts a different complexion on your social life this season," Lady Winter stated with relish.

"Mama, who but these creatures would accuse dear St. Charles of being a spy? We'll find it's all some dreadful error."

"Hmmph. Say what you will, you made a fool of yourself today. I can't go dragging you about till the scandal dies down. Wouldn't be any use, would it? I must have a practical return on any investment of time I make."

"Scandal? What scandal?" Annabella exclaimed.

"Why, you've spent the morning flinging yourself at the head of a young man who don't care a rush about you, and in front of the county. If there were nothing else to it, that would be enough, but with him a spy, you'll be twice as notorious as your cousin Mary within two days."

Annabella flushed. "I did nothing wrong. I merely believed in a young man who seemed quite honest to me." She directed a dark look at Mary. "As honest as *she* did not. And what makes you think the story will get out, Mama?"

"We must be prepared for any eventuality, Daughter. And while it ain't pleasant to think of you rattling around at home, there's no help for it. Unless—" A sudden thought appeared to strike Lady Winter "—you care to go to your Great-aunt Ismene in Bath. She's been writing again, asking you to come. There's no accounting for tastes."

"That old thing? I'd sooner perish of boredom here," said Annabella. From the way her eyes slid to Ramirez, Mary gathered that Annabella wouldn't give up a household with a young man in it—even a young man she despised as a foreigner—for all the great-aunts in the kingdom.

"Well," said Lady Winter, "keep it in your mind. If the scandal breaks, the Upper Rooms and Sydney Gardens might look a sight better than the four walls of our drawing room. I won't bother to take you about unless there's a decent chance of marrying you off, and that, my dear, is final. Good Lord! I've had one season of gadding already."

"It won't come to anything," Annabella said with scorn. "*I* didn't get my clothes ripped in Tattersall's."

As the sparring went on between the Winter ladies, Mary sighed over how small Sir Egbert's travelling coach seemed today. Ramirez's presence would have filled the carriage if the Winters had not, and his thigh pressed close to Mary's did nothing to help her forget he was there. From time to time he would smile at her and, as often as not, certain though she was that he had never been honest with her, she found herself smiling back.

To avoid this vexing behaviour, she directed her attention out the window. They were entering London. After a sparkling morning the day had turned cloudy. There was a hint of snow in the air, and a pervasive greyness made the streets look even gloomier than usual. Mary was surprised anew that she loved and longed to know better such an unattractive place. Bleak London certainly had nothing in common with the cities of the Peninsula. Yet it fascinated her as did no other place on earth.

When the carriage bowled into the City, Mary became extremely alert. She had never before visited the business part of town, and the solid temples of finance, built to last through any vicissitude, impressed her as much as her first sight of Carlton House had done. Before long, the coach drew up at a huge structure in Threadneedle Street.

"The Bank of England," said Ramirez, looking over his shoulder as he helped Mary alight. "An impressive place."

Captain Winter possessively took his daughter's arm, Ramirez assisted the Winter ladies, and the party went inside.

Once within the cavernous building, thick with scurrying clerks, Mary had no idea what to do. Should they demand their "Spanish treasure" of the first person who looked to be in authority? Suddenly the whole thing seemed silly, part of a fairy tale. A treasure box could not be here; practical things, ledgers and notes of hand, were the proper appurtenances of such a dignified bank, whereas a treasure ought to be buried in a cave along the seacoast.

The motley group, dressed in rumpled riding clothes and, in Captain Winter's case, a dowdy morning coat better suited to puttering round a cottage, received scant attention from those in charge until a sensible-looking, grey-haired man clad in conservative mouse-colour approached and gave a low, respectful bow. "Lord Ramirez! What a delightful surprise. Mr. Adolph will be pleased to see you—and your party."

Ramirez's smile gleamed as he made quick introductions. "This is Mr. Platt, a gentleman who has been of much assistance to me in my various endeavours."

Mary was astonished. Mr. Platt bowed deeply before her, and he was treating Antonio like royalty. A fencing master couldn't have business interests on a scale to make him important to bankers—could he?

The five visitors were led into the upper reaches and down a corridor. Mr. Platt stopped before one of the line of polished mahogany doors and opened it. "Lord Ramirez and a party to see you, sir," he said, speaking around the door.

He must have been pretty sure of their reception to bring them to the threshold before announcing them, was Mary's first thought. A voice acquiesced, and Mr. Platt bowed them in, shutting the door carefully behind them.

Here was a richly appointed office in what Mary supposed was the traditional, opulent City style: wine-red velvet draperies, gleaming dark wood furnishings, a case of leatherbound and gilt-trimmed books.

From behind the massive desk which formed the centrepiece of the room, a large gentleman rose. As grey as Mr. Platt, both in hair and clothing, this man exuded an aura of prosperity, of money newly minted.

"My dear Lord Ramirez! Come to see how your investments are coming along? You've nothing to fear, we've handled everything as you suggested, and matters are progressing. Ah! Forgive me. You've brought people to see me."

Ramirez smoothly introduced his wife, father-in-law, and the Winter ladies to Mr. Adolph, his "financial advisor."

Captain Winter, Lady Winter and Mr. Adolph exchanged a few pleasantries while Annabella stood by and scowled. Mary whispered into Ramirez's ear, "How much do fencing masters earn?"

Ramirez only smiled at her and patted her shoulder. He said to Mr. Adolph, "I've brought my family to you today for a certain very private purpose, Adolph. My wife, Lady Ramirez, is the possessor of a special piece of jewellery. Mary?"

Feeling very much on stage, Mary drew forth from the pocket of her habit the garnet necklace.

"My word!" said Mr. Adolph, staring. "The Spanish treasure. You don't say!"

"The very same," said Ramirez.

Mr. Adolph managed to look stern and apologetic at the same time. "There are many garnet necklaces, my dear sir. The key?"

Gently, Antonio took the necklace from Mary's hands and worked at the clasp. Mary watched closely and was astounded when the large garnet in its gold setting moved aside easily to reveal a tiny, oblong compartment. Inside was a miniscule key.

"You take it out, my dear," said Ramirez. "Your fingers are dainty enough for the job."

Stripping off her gloves, Mary reached into the compartment with one fingernail and extracted the small golden key.

Captain Winter had been watching these proceedings with a wary eye. "How did you know about that?" he demanded of Ramirez.

The younger man shrugged. "Several Spanish families were given the information. I believe you know why, sir."

Captain Winter frowned and said nothing. Mary looked curiously at her father but could evoke no response.

"A little key in the necklace! Fancy that," said Lady Winter. "You knew about this, Annabella?"

For once the talkative Miss Winter was at a loss for words. She merely shook her head and stared at the tiny key in Mary's hand.

"Well! This is an important day," said Mr. Adolph, and he rang a bell. When Mr. Platt entered, Adolph instructed him to go down to the vault and return with Item Fifty-three.

The man hastened upon his errand, and Mr. Adolph busied himself with setting chairs for his guests. Seeming to sense the restraint among the members of the party, he made no further allusions to the business at hand.

Mary sat in state in the best chair in the room. Mr. Adolph had pressed it upon "Lady Ramirez" and Mary, though afraid of disrespect to her aunt, hadn't known how to refuse. Despite her determination not to become overexcited, the thought of Mr. Platt entering with a huge chest full of gold couldn't but spark her imagination. Ramirez had given the necklace back to her, but she didn't return it to her pocket. She clutched it in one hand and the key in the other.

At length the door opened, and Mr. Platt came in. To Mary's surprise, he wasn't weighted down with a heavy strongbox, nor did any servants follow him with such an item. In one hand he held a small, paper-wrapped parcel. Mary looked at her father in wonder. He merely glared at her.

"How much treasure could be in that little packet?" Annabella said with a sneer. "Foreigners do exaggerate so, Mama."

"Hold your tongue," responded Lady Winter. Almost absently she raised her riding crop in her daughter's direction.

"Ah, thank you, Platt," said Adolph. The clerk left the room again, and Mr. Adolph approached Mary. "Would you do the honours, Madam?" He placed the little parcel in Mary's hand.

She unwrapped the paper to reveal a small gold box. The gold key went easily into its tiny lock, and Mary drew up the lid. It turned out to be lined in black velvet, and a letter was folded up inside, addressed to— Mary Winter!

"My goodness, this is Mama's handwriting," cried Mary, unfolding the paper.

"Drat that woman," grumbled the captain, "never could keep her mouth shut."

Mary smoothed out the single, crossed sheet and read the Spanish words. The missive was dated the very month before her mother's death.

My darling daughter,

You will perhaps be surprised to discover that I have chosen you to guard the safety of the treasure which has been placed in my charge. Knowing I have not long to live, I have already bequeathed to you my garnet necklace. When the time is ripe you will find that the small key in the clasp opens this letter to you.

In the bank where you will find these words, a great treasure has been sent for safekeeping. This is wealth donated not only by my family, but by several other leading houses who are dedicated to the cause of liberty for Spain, which we pray to achieve through our exiled monarch, Fernando. Those who will be made known to you, friends of our cause in England, will see the funds safely delivered to our people in Cadiz. I know, my daughter, that you have understood little of my secret life as a sympathizer against the absolutist regime, but that was for your safety. I have watched you grow into a strong woman, a woman who will keep the trust I have placed in her.

Your loving mama, etc.

When Mary looked up from the letter tears were rolling down her cheeks. Mama's handwriting brought back so many memories! She was not surprised to see that many pairs of eyes were fixed upon her in eager query.

"Oh, I'll read it," she said, and began to do just that. Mr. Adolph cleared his throat. Recalled to her surroundings, Mary translated from the Spanish as she read.

As she spoke the last words, Mary turned to her father. "Papa," she said sternly, "this money isn't mine. Did you know about this?"

Captain Winter was scowling into the distance. "Inez, I never could count on you to keep quiet." He turned, and his eyes met Mary's. "No, I didn't know about the letter. A tongue that ran at both ends, your mother had, even on paper. I always said so."

"Oh, Papa." Mary shook her head in disappointment. "You hoped to divert this money to us? It was raised for the cause!"

"Cause," said Captain Winter with a snort. "It's private money, and one of the families that raised it was your mother's. Do you say you have less right to it than those foolish Bourbons? Mary, even your husband here can tell you your mother's precious cause is a lot of fustian. Fernando's a Bourbon, ain't he? I met the young man, long ago at Court. Looked like a sly one to me. Can you imagine a king of Spain even having a working Parliament, let alone bowing to its demands?"

"You don't understand," said Ramirez. "He will return to the throne only if he accepts what the new constitution has to say. We wish to end the Inquisition, for one thing. What enlightened ruler can object to that?"

"Mary," said Captain Winter wearily, not looking at Ramirez, "I've been in Spain. We're fighting to give 'em back their king, ain't we? And the king the people want is the kind they've always had: the old-fashioned kind. Absolute. Takin' orders from no one.''

"Papa, what you're saying makes no difference. The money wasn't raised for me and you. We must see it go to this cause, no matter what you think of its chances for success.''

"You're throwin' it away,'' said her father, and he smashed his one fist against the arm of his chair. "Why don't we take a trip to Dover and fling it into the Channel? Or let another Frenchie steal it?''

"Captain,'' put in Ramirez, "your daughter has indicated that her choice is to follow your late wife's wishes. Would you deny her the happiness of serving her mother one last time?''

"I hate waste,'' muttered the captain.

Mary looked at her husband with shining eyes. "You were aware of all this, weren't you? You knew about the treasure, but you also realized it was to go to this cause—not to me.''

"It wasn't for me to tell you that,'' said Ramirez. "I hoped the news would be broken to you here, and so it has happened. We all imagined your mother must have written a letter.''

"And you believe, sir, that there is hope?'' Mary had to ask the question. "That the king will be brought back to Spain to rule like an English king?''

Ramirez looked serious. "Many of the enlightened families of Spain have their grave doubts; mine is one of them. But the alternative? To be ruled by the Bonapartes, to be nothing more than a part of the up-start Empire? Inconceivable. And you know as well as I and your father that the people of Spain are re-

solved to have their king back. They have been fighting to the death! We have no choice but to make this
attempt to bring Fernando to the throne, offering him
the constitution of Cadiz.''

"I understand," said Mary.

"I don't," snapped her father. "Useless lot of
foolery, if you ask me. I've seen a lot of Spain, and
I—"

"Strange talk, sir, from a captain in Wellington's
army," said Ramirez.

"Hmmph! It's because I've served that I know what
I'm talking about. Oh, get Boney out of there by all
means. Wish I could be there to help. But your dreams
of a new era for Spain are doomed, lad. Doomed."

"Politics!" put in Lady Winter with a snort. "Never
could abide such talk. Annabella, you can see right
enough that the St. Charles boy must have been a
Frenchie. A treasure for the Spanish cause! Just the
thing for a French spy to try to get his hands on. Wait
till we tell Sir Egbert you've been duped."

Annabella made a little sound of frustration. "I, a
dupe! What about Mary, giving a lot of wealth away?
Well, I would like to see this treasure everyone is
making so much fuss about."

Ramirez turned to Mary. "Wouldn't you like to see
it, too?"

She shrugged. "I don't really care. Is it possible,
Antonio, for us to have a talk?"

"I thought you'd never ask," said Ramirez, holding out a hand to her. At that very moment the door
opened, and a stout clerk wheeled a massive, leatherbound chest into the room.

CHAPTER FOURTEEN

"HERE IT IS," said Mr. Adolph proudly, thumping the dusty wooden casket once it had been set in the middle of the room. "Just as it was when it was deposited with us three years ago."

Everyone had sprung from their chairs when the chest was brought into the room. Mary found herself edging closer to Ramirez as the banker extracted a bunch of keys from a drawer in his desk and bent down to the casket. He flung wide the lid.

Mary gasped, and her father groaned as if in pain. Annabella gave a squeal and ran to the chest to sift its contents through her fingers.

"Fancy that," said Lady Winter, her eyes fixed on the mounds of money and jewels. "Pirates' gold."

"Pirates' gold, indeed," Ramirez agreed, laughing. "What a fine sight. Some of the doubloons are from my father, and that long box contains the Mondego emeralds, my mother's offering."

Annabella had opened the box and was fondling the emeralds in question. "Oh, I would look so *very* well in these. Mama, could we buy them from the—from whoever owns them?"

Lady Winter didn't dignify the suggestion with an answer, but she approached the chest for a closer look.

Gold and unset stones and silver filled the large casket nearly to the brim. Mary could see, at second glance, that there was a box or two in the lower part of the chest probably packed with some family heirloom. There were also various leather and silk purses tucked in among the loose coins. The liberals of Spain had contributed a treasure indeed.

"What a waste," moaned Captain Winter. He struggled down to his knees, heedless of his pantaloons, and ran his hand through the coins. Annabella, on her own knees beside him, was totally given up to the rapt contemplation of the treasure.

Mr. Adolph tried to help by pointing out the value of some of the items; Captain Winter only sighed more deeply, but Annabella's interest was piqued, and she treated the banker to a dose of her charm while her mother stood by and shook her head at her daughter's every simper.

Meanwhile Ramirez drew Mary aside, between a set of bookshelves and the rich velvet window drapes. "My dearest, aren't we forgetting something? The mystery of the treasure is revealed, and it will soon be on its way to help our cause. There are so many things I couldn't tell you before. Your uncle, as you may have guessed, is my superior."

"Uncle Egbert?" said Mary in astonishment. "You—and he—are agents for the government?"

"He has never wanted his family to know, but he gave me leave to tell you. That is why he and I have spent what must have looked like a suspicious amount of time together. But the most important thing you must understand is that I didn't marry you for your dowry. Are you convinced at last?"

Mary gazed at him. "Papa was so angry that I'd married you, and your behaviour over the necklace seemed to confirm that he was right about you, once I'd heard the full story of the treasure. I had no way of knowing that it wasn't mine, and therefore yours. I'm very sorry for doubting your motives. I've always wondered why you married me, and an economic reason seemed to make the most sense. You are so very good at flattery, Antonio. So very practiced. It never seemed real to me."

"Darling Mary, I can see I'll have my work cut out for me. As your husband—as your real husband—I know I can make you believe in the truth at last. That I married you because I was falling in love with you."

"On one day's acquaintance?" He was flattering her again, and she wouldn't stand for it. "Come, sir, you can't expect any rational creature to believe that story."

"You forget," said Ramirez, "I had seen you before the day of our marriage, at Holland House. Ever since that night I had been thinking of the lovely young woman I spoke with so briefly. I knew who you were, for Lord Holland told me, but nothing of where you lived, how to find you, how you might be circumstanced. I had resolved to ask Lord Holland for your direction, no matter how bold and unseemly that might look. When I was lucky enough to save you in the street that day, it seemed nothing short of a miracle."

"I—" Mary caught herself; she had been about to say that she understood, that when she had seen him again, after thinking of him for days, it had been a dream come true. He couldn't have felt that same attraction—could he?

"You can't call it love," she insisted. "If you were, well, glad to see me again, that still wasn't reason enough to marry me."

Ramirez shook his head, smiling at her as though she had said something very foolish. "Have it your way, then. But love might grow, don't you think? Could we try?" He raised her hand to his lips as he spoke. Then he drew her close and kissed her: a lingering, questioning kiss.

Mary answered that question with her heart, returning the kiss with more passion than she had thought she had in her. Her riding hat fell off, and she felt Antonio's hands stroking her back, moving lower down. Forgetting they were in the office of a bank, in front of several of her relations, she kissed him fervently.

"Er, Lord Ramirez," said Mr. Adolph with a cough, "I hate to interrupt, but there is a question of some of your concerns, now you are here. We're nearing the end of the business day, though naturally I shall stay as long as your convenience requires. And we must close up the chest . . ."

"Oh! Forgive us. Adolph, you may wish me happy," said Ramirez. He did not turn to look at the banker, but kept his attention on the woman who rested safely within his arms.

"Ahem! By all means, sir, but I understood that your marriage was of long standing?"

"On the contrary, it's just beginning," returned Ramirez. "Ah, business. You're right, sir. We must not forget where we are. Though this would be an excellent time to familiarize Lady Ramirez and her father with some of my activities, the other ladies would doubtless be bored.''

''Oh, don't be too sure,'' said Lady Winter tartly.

''What's all this faradiddle?'' put in Captain Winter, rising with difficulty from his worshipful position before the treasure chest. ''You, sir, are a fencing master and a ruined aristocrat. If you're a saving sort, I'm glad, for perhaps my daughter won't starve too quickly, but how much could you have put by?''

Ramirez bowed. ''I'm a fairly astute fellow, Captain. I've used my connections with the important men I meet through my fencing studio. More than one gentleman of the ton has dealings in business, you know, though such sordid matters are kept quiet in society. I've picked up some valuable hints as to the right investments to make. There is also—occasionally—some slight recompense for services rendered to the Foreign Office. I've invested it all, and I've done quite well. There is enough to keep all three of us in comfort.''

''Lord Ramirez understates the case, Captain Winter,'' said Mr. Adolph. ''His is one of the fastest growing piles in the City, if you'll forgive the crass terminology.''

''You don't say,'' said Captain Winter, eyes bulging.

''Wait,'' said Mary. She turned to Ramirez. ''If you've been wealthy all along, why did you come to live on charity at my relations' estate? And why didn't you tell me at the time of our marriage that you weren't a pauper?''

"You aren't the only one who would have disliked to be married for money, my dear. And as for living at Woodbank Hall, it was the most convenient way, my superiors and I agreed, for me to have the means to unmask the French agent who rumour had it was lurking in the neighbourhood. Lord Burnham, you see, was taken in by false letters of introduction."

"And to think that Uncle Egbert—" Mary was beginning, with a smile at her quiet uncle's double life as an agent of the Crown, when Ramirez shook his head at her and put a finger to her lips. Lady Winter was hovering close by.

Mary coughed to punctuate her sentence.

"And now, Lady Winter," said Ramirez, bowing, "if you would excuse your niece and me? We have unfinished business." Without further ado he pulled Mary back into his arms.

"Well!" Lady Winter beamed on the united couple. "Don't say I didn't warn you, Mary. Told you you're fond of him already."

THE PARTY THE WINTERS GAVE for Mary and her husband was the most talked-of affair of the Christmas season, causing even those who still disapproved of Mary to sigh over the happy sight of two lovers united in marriage. Such a well-suited couple had never been seen in that part of Berkshire, everyone agreed in perfect charity, for at last the attention of the gossip-mongers was off Mary and her escapade at Tattersall's. Another titillating story had taken the place of that old news.

Annabella stood fuming in a corner of the drawing room on the night of the party. She was quite alone.

No young man had come near her since that story of "Miss A. W. of B--shire's" alleged engagement to "an unidentified young man, a traitor to England," had appeared in the gossip column of the *Gazette*.

"Ooh!" she said in frustration when the tenth former suitor passed her by with only a nervous half bow. "This is unbearable." Pausing only to finish the plate of macaroons and jellies she had in her hands, her third of the evening, she swept out of the room and up the stairs, holding her head high and trying not to care that not one person that evening had commented on her exquisite new gown of peach sarcenet. She had never worn a neck so low, and everyone must have noticed.

Well, things would be different once she was with Aunt Ismene in Bath. Annabella was planning to make that visit as soon as the snowy roads permitted, and she defied any heart in Bath to remain whole once confronted by her splendid looks and sophisticated London wardrobe.

When she was in the first-floor gallery, a little imp of mischief poked at Annabella's shoulder. Ramirez and Mary, in true newlywed fashion, had retired early to the Queen's Chambers. Annabella believed they had done so merely as a pretense, for she couldn't feature the handsome Ramirez being truly captivated by quiet cousin Mary, as he had seemed to be since that day at the bank.

With an air of long practise, Annabella cupped her hands over one ear and placed her head to the door of the Queen's Bedchamber. She wasn't trying to eavesdrop; she merely wanted to make sure that dear Mary was passing another peaceful night on her solitary couch.

"WHAT WAS THAT?" whispered Mary. Fairly jumping out of Antonio's arms, she let her suddenly frightened eyes dart about the firelit shadows of the bedroom. The sound outside the door had been very like a girl squealing, followed by running feet, and then a splintering crash.

Ramirez kissed his wife and rose from the bed, casually wrapping a dressing gown round himself. "I'll see."

Mary sighed in contentment as she watched him stride so confidently across the room. He opened the door. To her surprise, he went a few steps down the corridor. She heard him laugh. Well, one of the inebriated gentlemen from the party might have lost his way and be causing a ruckus. Perhaps that feminine shriek had been one of the maids being pinched, or worse. Mary could hear quite a commotion out in the gallery now, but she couldn't follow Antonio to see what was going on. She was quite unclothed.

Her husband came back into the room and shut the door just as Mary's curiosity was becoming more than she could bear. "Well, what was it?" she asked eagerly.

He shrugged, casting aside his robe. "I am so glad, my dear, that the priest was able to join us this morning. It might mean nothing to the laws of this country, but I wouldn't have felt so truly married otherwise. Let me see, where did we leave off? Ah, yes."

"Please. I'm curious."

"I know, it is one of your more endearing qualities. Didn't you tell me you wondered about this—and this—"

"Antonio! What was going on out there?"

"Oh, that. Your poor cousin Annabella must have seen a mouse or something that distressed her when she came upstairs. She was rushing back down to the main floor when she ran into the dog gates. Don't worry. A couple of the footmen are helping her to her feet, the gates can certainly be repaired, and James says it's all his fault for closing them behind the young lady."

"He had to, by Lady Winter's strict orders, though Annabella never does remember," said Mary. "And now do let's stop talking about Cousin Annabella, my love."

"I thought you'd never come to your senses, *my* love," was her husband's quick response.

And Mary didn't think about her cousin even once for the rest of the night.

Harlequin Regency Romance™

COMING NEXT MONTH

#23 PRESCOTT'S LADY by Clarice Peters
Lady Eleanor Whiting and Lord Peter Prescott had
been engaged until Eleanor discovered that Peter had
not given up the mistress he had promised he would.
True to form, Eleanor returned his engagement ring in
a bit o'muslin and created a public scandal that made
Peter the laughingstock of the ton. When
circumstances throw them together three years later,
the legendary battle begins anew, but this time the
battle concludes with a turn of events that surprises
them both!

#24 LORD TOM by Patricia Wynn
When Lord Tom Harleston promised Susan
Johnstone's father to get her safely back to England,
he was already half in love. Although Susan was
reluctant to risk Tom's reputation on such a
dangerous adventure, she succumbed to his
enthusiasm and twinkling brown eyes. But once
back in England, another adventure began. One that
could reveal their true identities and send Susan to
the gallows....

You'll flip . . . your pages won't!
Read paperbacks *hands-free* with

Book Mate · I

The perfect "mate" for all your romance paperbacks

Traveling • Vacationing • At Work • In Bed • Studying
• Cooking • Eating

Perfect size for all standard paperbacks, this wonderful invention makes reading a pure pleasure! Ingenious design holds paperback books OPEN and FLAT so even wind can't ruffle pages — leaves your hands free to do other things. Reinforced, wipe-clean vinyl-covered holder flexes to let you turn pages without undoing the strap . . . supports paperbacks so well, they have the strength of hardcovers!

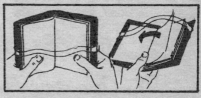

Pages turn WITHOUT opening the strap

SEE-THROUGH STRAP

Reinforced back stays flat

Built in bookmark

BOOK MARK

BACK COVER HOLDING STRIP

10 x 7¼ opened
Snaps closed for easy carrying, too